"Why did you call me a 'nice' girl?"

"Well..." He _____ ever _____ ing to study the vo_____ _____ on all three cushion_____ _____ce."

Something i_____ _____dsome hunk would never, ever be attracted to someone like her.

"I am nice, really nice, so why don't gorgeous single guys like *you* want nice girls like *me*?"

"Miss—Julie, I don't know you well enough to—"

"I'm sick of being a good girl and getting dumped on. I'm changing my image." Her shoulders slumped, and he was afraid she'd get emotional on him. "But I don't have a clue where to begin."

"Maybe I can give you a few pointers..."

"Sure, that'd be nice."

"I'll tell you what's wrong with nice girls," he muttered under his breath. "They make guys like me feel like jerks."

Jennifer Drew is a mother-daughter writing team who live in Wisconsin and West Virginia respectively. Before they became partners, Mum was a columnist for an antiques newspaper and her daughter was a journalist and teacher. Both are thrilled to be writing together.

THE BAD-GIRL BRIDE

BY
JENNIFER DREW

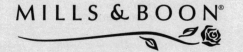

MILLS & BOON®

To Joan

MILLS & BOON and MILLS & BOON with the Rose Device are registered trademarks of the publisher.

First published in Great Britain 1999
Harlequin Mills & Boon Limited,
Eton House, 18-24 Paradise Road, Richmond, Surrey TW9 1SR

© Pamela Hanson and Barbara Andrews 1998

ISBN 0 263 81748 2

Set in Times Roman 10½ on 12 pt
01-9908-44029 C1

Printed and bound in Spain
by Litografía Rosés, S.A., Barcelona

1

Wedding Dress For Sale. Size 6. Never worn.
Best offer. 555-1221.

"I'm here about the wedding dress."

Julie Myers's intercom distorted voices in strange
ways, but this was the first time it had made someone
sound like Kevin Costner. She hadn't noticed that
sexy drawl in her visitor's voice when she'd talked to
him on the phone. Maybe she'd been too eager to sell
THE DRESS to notice.

She had second thoughts about buzzing him up, but
how many psycho killers cruised the classifieds looking for wedding gowns? Her ad had run for three
days, and this guy was the only person who'd called.

"You're Tom Brunswick?" She read his name
from the notepad by the phone.

"That's me."

"Come on up."

She pushed the button to let him into the vestibule
and opened her door a crack, waiting for him to climb
the two flights to her apartment.

What kind of man bought a wedding dress for his
fiancée? If he was bargain hunting, he'd come to the
right place. Like the ad said, she was open to all of-

fers, even if it meant losing money to get the wretched thing out of her closet.

From her vantage point, she saw the top of his head first: golden blond hair with dark highlights, parted in the middle and long enough to look unruly. An instant later he climbed the last step and any resemblance to a shaggy dog ended at his hairline. He was a genuine hunk, six feet of muscle and sex appeal packed into a worn brown leather bomber jacket and tight faded jeans.

"You're Julie?" He glanced at a slip of paper in his hand. "Julie Myers?"

"Yes."

"Do you want to bring the dress out here?" He eyed her through the door crack she'd been using as a spy hole.

"Oh, no, sorry." Why did gorgeous men always make her act like a total klutz? "Just let me take the chain off."

She unintentionally slammed the door in his face with a loud bang, fumbled with the chain and opened it again, relieved that he was still there.

"Come in. It's here on the couch."

He stepped into the living room and slowly appraised her from the dark bangs on her forehead to her feet clad in heavy socks and wide-strap sandals.

"You look about right."

"Right for what?"

He circled for a better look, and she imagined his dark brown laser eyes dissolving her clothes. Should she run, scream, or play it cool?

"You're in better shape than Tina, but I guess it won't matter. Looks like that skirt has plenty of room."

"Oh, you mean I'm about the same size as your fiancée!"

This was even more awkward than she'd imagined. Wasn't there some rule about the groom never seeing the bride's dress before the ceremony?

"I don't have a fiancée."

He walked over to the gown she'd tried to display artfully on her flowered chintz couch.

"Then why…" She clamped her jaw shut, realizing she should stifle her curiosity in the interest of selling the dress.

"My sister's the one who needs it."

"You're buying it for your sister?"

"Yeah, my twin actually." He rubbed his hands on the sides of his jeans, then lifted one sleeve of the gown, seemingly checking the length without touching the beaded bodice. "She had a dress being altered, but there was a fire at the bridal shop. Heavy smoke and water damage, with no chance of replacing it in time."

"How awful," Julie murmured, unable to tell whether he liked her dress or not. He gingerly lifted the hem with two fingers, looking as uncomfortable as a young boy caught looking up his teacher's skirt.

"It's nice of you to help her find a replacement."

"I just happened to notice your ad when I was looking for Bulls tickets in the classifieds."

"When is the wedding?"

She wanted to say something that would persuade him to buy it, but he looked at her again with smoky brown eyes that intimidated her.

"This weekend."

"She must be desperate."

"She's a flight attendant, snowed in at the Denver

airport. Her flight is on indefinite hold, so she has to keep herself available. No chance to shop.''

'''She must be frantic, trying to get here for the wedding, and she doesn't even have a gown.''

Julie tried to imagine a female version with his dark bedroom eyes, rumpled blond hair and dynamite good looks. If the sister looked anything like her brother, the groom would marry her if she wore sweats.

''You said this has never been worn?''

''No—I mean yes, that's what I said. It's brand-new. I couldn't take it back because there's no return on wedding gowns.''

''You were going to wear it?''

''Yes.''

''What happened?'' he asked casually.

His tone made it clear he was just being polite and didn't really care, but his question still bothered her. No one had been surprised when popular, outgoing Brad Wilson dumped quiet, unexciting Julie, but it still rankled to admit she'd been jilted on the morning of her wedding.

''The groom met the girl of his dreams at his bachelor party. Of course, she was only working as a stripper to put herself through college.''

''Hey, I'm sorry.''

He probably meant he was sorry he'd asked.

''It was six months ago. I'm over it. Of course, my parents had to pay for the hall they rented, and my aunt Ellen doesn't know what to do with the four pounds of hand-molded pastel mints in her freezer. Your sister doesn't need any candy wedding bells, does she?'' she said as a joke, but it fizzled.

''Uh, no thanks. About the dress—are you sure you

want to sell it? I mean, a nice girl like you is sure to get another chance to wear it.''

"I need the room in my closet.''

She didn't tell him how fervently she wanted to get it out of her apartment, out of the suburb of Roseville, preferably out of the state of Illinois.

"Why did you call me a 'nice' girl?''

"Well...'' He averted his eyes, pretending to study the voluminous skirt spread out on all three cushions of the couch. "You seem nice.''

Something inside her snapped. This handsome hunk would never, ever, be attracted to someone like her. She wasn't flashy enough. He wouldn't take a second look if he walked into the florist shop where she worked. She had nothing whatsoever to lose by asking him The Big Question. It might be her only chance to bump heads with the truth.

"I am nice, really nice, so why don't gorgeous single guys like *you* want nice girls like *me?*''

"Miss—Julie, I don't know you well enough to—''

"No! I want to know. What's wrong with being a nice girl?''

"Just because some jerk broke up with you—''

"Dumped me. He practically jilted me at the altar, then he tried to tell me I'm too good for him.''

"You probably are.'' He shrugged and lifted the other lacy sleeve of the gown. "I think my sister will like this.''

"Fine. You can have it for a hundred less than I paid—the receipt's on the coffee table. But only if you tell me what's wrong with being a nice girl. I bet you've broken up with more than one woman and used the same lame excuse that she was too good for you.''

"I don't think I've ever said that...exactly."

Tom picked up the wrinkled pink receipt and realized what a bargain the dress was, but its owner
wasn't exactly easy to deal with. In fact, she'd hit a
sore spot. He'd used precisely those words just days
ago to break up with a cute but marriage-minded redhead.

"Sometimes the chemistry just isn't right. Or the
timing is wrong," he suggested, wondering why he
was letting her prick his conscience. He wasn't the
love-'em-and-leave-'em type. He just enjoyed his
freedom too much to saddle himself with a wife. His
unfinished furniture store was finally starting to be
moderately successful, and he wanted to enjoy life.

"Bad chemistry," she said scornfully, wrinkling
her cute little nose and staring at him with big blue
eyes. "Next you'll tell me men do like nice girls—
as pals."

He shifted from one foot to the other, torn between
wanting to cheer her up and wanting to get away from
those rosy lips puckered into a kissable *O*. He didn't
think she wanted to hear that "bad girls" were more
fun—and less likely to get a gleam in their eyes
whenever they passed a jewelry store.

"About the dress—"

"I'm sick of being a good girl and getting dumped
on. I'm changing my image." Her shoulders slumped,
and he was afraid she'd get emotional on him. "But
I don't have a clue where to begin."

Why was she asking him for advice? Tom wondered. Giving advice on "relationships" wasn't his
strong suit. His common sense and self-preservation
instincts told him to leave it alone, but her big baby-

blues were reeling him in. She needed help—boy, did she need it! What the heck—advice was cheap.

"You don't need to change your image. Just your attitude."

"How?"

He had one foot in quicksand. It was definitely time to fall back and regroup. This woman had enough assets to get attention anywhere: long, dark, silky hair; luscious curves that couldn't be concealed by jeans and a bulky red sweatshirt; an adorable face with a sexy mouth.

"You're cute. You come across as open, caring...." He nearly said "nice." "What you need to do is be more aloof. Be coy, unavailable."

And don't ask strangers for lovelorn advice, he wanted to add.

"My mother told me all that when I first started dating, but you make it sound like you're leaking tribal secrets. I am coy! I am aloof! It's not my fault I'm still available."

If she was coy or aloof, he was the Abominable Snowman. In fact, everything he'd seen so far showed she was just the opposite: forthright, sweet, vulnerable—a very nice girl, one a guy could take home to meet his parents. She was exactly the kind he *wasn't* looking for.

"It's the best I can do," he said. "When the chemistry is right..."

She sighed. "I almost flunked chemistry in high school. So, do you want the dress?"

Her tone told him his advice had fallen flat.

"Yeah, it's nice. I'm pretty sure my sister will want it, but I'd better check with her first. She's supposed to call me tonight. Could you possibly hold it until tomorrow?''

"Sure, why not?"

"Hey, cheer up, there's a lot to be said for not getting married too young. You're only—what? Twenty-one?''

"Twenty-five.''

"Still a kid.'' He grinned, but she didn't grin back. "I'm a year past the big three-oh and light-years away from taking the big step.''

"I'll hold the dress until you check with your sister. If the price is a problem—''

"No, it's fine.'' He'd be embarrassed to buy it for any less; the girl had been dumped, after all. "Maybe I can give you a few pointers when I come to get it.''

"Sure, that'd be nice.''

She walked him to the door, then closed it behind him before he reached the stairs.

"I'll tell you what's wrong with nice girls,'' he muttered under his breath. "They make guys like me feel like jerks.''

Tom made several stops on his way home. Finally he entered his apartment and checked the answering machine. It was late, nearly midnight, but he had to run through all the messages in case his sister had called from Denver. He had no intention of returning any of Bambi's calls, but missing one from Greta was a disappointment. He'd been wanting to get together with her since they'd met on a ski weekend.

Tina called just as he was crawling into bed, and her first few words told him how edgy she was. The sooner this wedding business was over, the happier he'd be.

"Describe it to me," she demanded. "Is it pure white or ivory?"

"It looked white to me. There are little beads on top," he said, not immune to the note of panic in his sister's voice.

"Pearls? What about lace? It isn't too fussy, is it?"

"It's nice, and it's never been worn. The girl who's selling it was jilted the day of the wedding. She's about your size and height, only not as bottom-heavy. But there's enough skirt to hide the whole wedding party."

"I may have gotten Mom's hips, but at least I got her brains. What if this girl sells the dress to someone else? Tom, you idiot! Why didn't you just buy it? You know I'm desperate!"

"Don't worry. She's holding it for me."

"Oh, sure. If she gets a better offer, she'll turn it down in case you decide to buy it. Did you give her a deposit?"

"Never thought of it."

He tried to be tolerant of Tina's prewedding jitters, but his twin was beginning to annoy him. He'd never tell her—and he hated admitting it to himself—but he wouldn't mind going back for another look at Julie Myers. He felt sorry about what had happened to her, of course, but she was something of a novelty. Nice girls with bodies like hers weren't all that plentiful in his experience, especially not ones as easy on the eyes as the jilted bride. She'd probably make a terrific wife for some guy who wanted her in his bed permanently. Strings like that just weren't for him.

"Buy it, Tom," Tina insisted. "I can't get married without a dress. Don't blow this."

* * *

He called Julie from the store early the next morning.

"My sister wants the dress," he said. "I can come over anytime today. Business is slow in January."

"Don't I know it," she agreed. "All I've done this month is send flowers to hospitals and funeral homes."

"Oh." The vision of sick beds and coffins didn't square with his memory of long spiky lashes and blushing cheeks.

"I work for a florist," she explained. "I have to leave for work now. Come for the dress anytime tonight."

"Your place is on my way home. I'll be there shortly after six."

He got to her apartment complex early and sat in the van shivering while he waited because he hadn't taken time to fill his nearly empty gas tank.

At one minute after six he buzzed her apartment and identified himself. She sounded like Minnie Mouse on the intercom, which was good. Her squeaky, "Come on up," was reassuring; she was a nice girl but not one he'd ever take seriously.

This time she let him in without the peeping-through-the-crack routine. Her cheeks were pink, as though she'd just rushed in from the cold, and she seemed a little breathless.

"I left it out in case you want another look," she said, turning to lead him to the couch in the snug little room done in shades of bright yellow and muted green. The end tables she'd painted a nice moss green looked like a style he carried in the store.

"Nice tables," he said, wondering why he hadn't

noticed them the first time he'd been here. Her cheeks got even pinker.

"Thanks. I bought them in an unfinished furniture store and painted them myself."

"Not the Unfinished Gallery on Euclid?"

"Yes, how did you know?"

"That's my store. You did a good job. A lot of people slap on paint without sanding or priming, then wonder why it looks shoddy."

All of which had nothing to do with getting a dress for his sister, he realized, deciding it was dumb to feel so darned pleased because she'd bought a couple of his tables.

"I guess you bought them from one of my clerks," he added, wondering if he could possibly have seen her before and forgotten.

"An older woman. I remember people pretty well."

"My mother helps out sometimes."

"She was very nice." Julie grinned.

"Is something funny?"

"I shouldn't tell you."

"Nothing my mother does can surprise me."

"She mentioned something about wishing her son would find a nice girl."

He groaned, and she giggled self-consciously.

"I shouldn't have told you," she said. "It was only small talk. I may have mentioned I wanted the tables for a new apartment after—"

"About the dress." He wasn't going to give her a chance to reminisce about the wedding that wasn't. "I'll pay cash so you won't have to worry about my check."

"You don't look like the bad-check type."

"Thank you," he said with mock gravity. "I'm glad my good character is shining through."

"I'll put the gown in the plastic bag that came with it."

"That'd be ni—good, thanks."

What he'd really like was to have her model it for him. Or even better, he'd like to watch her change into it. She was wearing a short green wool skirt that confirmed his earlier assessment: she had a fantastic behind. He wondered if she wore those lacy little panties that looked like decoration for a valentine. And a matching see-through bra would be nice, too—very nice, considering how well she'd fill the cups.

If she really wanted some rules on how to be a bad girl, number one was: Dress the part, beginning with some really sexy lingerie.

She went into the bedroom and came back with a transparent plastic bag and a padded satin hanger.

"I'll try not to wrinkle it." She looked around as though she'd lost something.

"Is there a problem?"

"No, I'm just deciding how to do this."

"Can I help?" He didn't wait for an answer. "Getting big things into tight places is my specialty."

"I can manage," she said frostily.

He realized what he'd said, and it was his turn to flush. "I was talking about furniture—you know, packing a lot into the van. Here, give me the bag, and you bring the dress. If we do it on the bed, everything will be fine. I mean, that way the dress won't drag on the floor."

He didn't give her a choice. Ducking into the bedroom, he spread the bag on her quilted patchwork spread and pulled open the zipper, trying not to inhale the teasingly feminine scent of the room. She had good taste in perfume, if that was what he was smelling.

"Bad-girl rule number two. Never let a guy see you're scared," he said when she lingered in the doorway with the dress across her arms.

"I'm not scared! I'm trying to decide the best way to do this." She circled the bed so she was on the side opposite from him. "What's rule number one?"

"I'll keep that to myself for now."

He grinned, thinking how much fun it would be to shock her with advice on lingerie, but he didn't want to be thrown out of her apartment without the dress. Tina would skin him alive if he bungled the deal.

The bed was a single, and they nearly bumped heads when they both bent over to ease the gown into the bag.

"Don't let the skirt catch in the zipper," she warned when he started to pull up the tab.

"I'll let you do it," he said.

He straightened and watched the top of her head as she carefully closed the opening.

"Why don't you come to the wedding with me?" He almost looked around to see if those words had really come from him. He'd surprised himself more than he had her—and she looked shell-shocked. Sure, he enjoyed looking at her—what man wouldn't?—but he didn't want to adopt her. It wasn't his style to play Big Daddy checking out the studs for his little girl.

"Your sister's wedding?" She was stalling, and he held his breath, silently urging her to decline.

"I don't have a date." No need to mention he'd just dumped her. "A lot of single guys will be there. You might meet someone."

He made a big show of gathering up the dress, regretting his impulsive invitation but expecting her to turn him down. The last thing a jilted bride wanted was to watch someone else get married in her gown.

"Sure, why not? I survived my cousin's wedding last month, and no one at your sister's will be whispering 'Poor Julie' behind my back."

She made it sound almost as much fun as a root canal, but he didn't see any way to renege. It might be just what she needed—although he didn't have a clue why he should care.

"If you're sure…" he said, giving her a chance to back out.

"Unless you want to change your mind?" she asked timidly.

"No, not at all. You'll be helping me out. My mother has four sisters dedicated to finding a nice girl for me. You'll keep them at bay by showing up with me."

"If I do go with you—"

"I thought it was settled." He followed her back to the living room and pulled the envelope of cash out of his jacket pocket. "For the dress."

"Thank you. I don't quite know how to ask this…." She'd been thinking about it ever since she'd met him, but actually asking out loud was a lot harder.

"Straight-out works for me."

"If I go with you—"

"That's settled. I'll pick you up early because I'm ushering. Say around two-thirty."

"I just wondered if you'd give me a few lessons on how to attract a man?"

She was blushing so furiously, he didn't have the heart to make a joke of it.

"Look, I'm probably the wrong person to give you advice."

"Think of it as tutoring. I haven't had a date since the breakup. It's like I'm wearing the sign Little Miss No Fun."

"You're being awfully hard on yourself."

"Just an inside joke. My brother used to call me that because I never got in trouble."

"Look, maybe the wedding is a bad idea."

"You're uninviting me?"

"No, no way." He was the one who should be wearing a Kick Me sign!

"I'm thinking of a business deal—an exchange. You said you were looking for Bulls tickets in the classifieds. My ex-fiancé gave me a pair of season passes as an engagement present. Of course, he intended to use one of the seats himself, but so far he hasn't had enough nerve to ask me to return them. You don't have to guarantee results. Just give me some pointers, and the tickets are yours."

"I'm more than willing to buy them from you."

"They're not for sale."

He couldn't hold back a silly grin. Season tickets just for playing Cupid? When his friends saw Julie, they'd probably do the job for him. He knew lots of guys who weren't afraid of the big "C" word. Some were actually looking for a woman to marry.

"This is the craziest deal I've ever been offered," he said.

"Does that mean you'll do it?"

"I may not be much help."

"No, but if my ex-fiancé gets up enough courage to try to buy back the tickets, I'd love to tell him what I did with them."

He took a deep breath. She deserved a bit of sweet revenge. He liked her more, knowing she wasn't quite perfect.

"It's a deal." He stuck out his hand.

She shook it.

"See ya."

Julie leaned against the door after he left, not trusting her legs to carry her to a chair. She was exhausted. Men like Tom always made her tongue-tied and flustered. He was so far out of her league, the two of them belonged on different planets.

She couldn't believe he'd agreed to her crazy proposal. She couldn't believe she'd had the nerve to suggest it.

She especially couldn't believe he'd asked her to the wedding before she even mentioned the tickets.

But she did know exactly what she was going to do with the envelope of money in her hand.

2

"I'd love to go, but I have plans," Julie said, the phone propped on her shoulder as she put the final touches on a basket of silk flowers she was taking to the wedding as her gift.

"Plans? You're telling your best friend since third grade you have plans?" Karen asked. "Sounds like a date to me."

"Just a wedding."

"Why didn't you say so? Who's getting married?"

Julie let the phone slip, but caught it before it clattered to the floor. Any other time she'd be eager to tell Karen about her date, but how could she explain Tom? She still couldn't believe she'd asked him to help her attract a man.

"Just a friend of a friend. If you can wait until tomorrow, we'll go to the mall and I'll tell you all about it."

"My mother's expecting me for dinner. Tell me more about this wedding. Is the friend you're going with a male?"

"Just a guy who needed a date at the last minute."

"Julie, that's great! Even if it doesn't work out—"

"It won't. It's more like a business arrangement.

If I get home early enough, I'll call and tell you how it went. I have to hang up now. Talk to you later.''

Either Karen's curiosity had heated up the plastic, or she was running a fever. Her palm was sweaty as she dropped the receiver back into the cradle.

She focused on the wedding present, but before she could finish the basket of flowers, the phone rang again.

''Julie, this is Tom Brunswick.''

She was so sure he was calling to cancel, she jumped in to call it off herself.

''If you've changed your mind…'' She could see the pattern: bachelor party, stripper and canceled date. She was doomed to sit home alone while every man she ever met succumbed to the charms of a half-naked dancer.

''Why should I? I'm just sorry I haven't had time to give you a few pointers before we go. I got in a big shipment yesterday and didn't have time to call you. Then I had to go to the rehearsal dinner and the bachelor party afterward.''

''I won't hold you to it if you've had second thoughts.'' *Like I have,* she wanted to add.

''No way, we have a deal. I just wanted to give you a few basics before we go—you know, hints like always laugh at a guy's jokes, but don't overdo it. The same with smiling. Make him think you're grinning because you have a secret.''

''Tom, I don't think we should do this—''

''And don't hide in a corner with some loser, hanging on everything he says just so you don't have to stand around alone. Alone is good. It shows you have self-confidence. It means you don't need to hang with a pack of women to feel secure. And whatever you do, don't act desperate. You're the shopper, not the merchandise.''

''I get it! I knew all that in junior high!''

''Sorry. I'll be more helpful after I've seen you in action. I need to know what you're doing wrong. It's hard to coach you until I see your technique.''

''I don't have one.''

She'd asked for his tutoring, but it made her feel as though she was in over her head. Maybe asking him to help could be written off as temporary insanity.

''I'll see you at two-thirty,'' he promised.

''Thanks for boosting my confidence,'' she said into the dead receiver.

She might feel like a wallflower, but she didn't intend to look like one. She'd invested some of the money from her wedding gown in a terrific little dress on sale at Woodfield Mall. It cost more per ounce than anything she'd ever owned, but it was skimpy enough to weigh on a letter scale.

Ten minutes before Tom was due, she looked at her image in the full-length mirror on her closet door and saw a stranger in a long-sleeved, rose-red dress draped to leave one shoulder bare. The hem ended at mid-thigh, proving she didn't have to be tall to have the leggy supermodel look.

Maybe she'd wear her coat during the ceremony.

Or maybe she wouldn't.

A bad girl would flaunt it all, from her upswept hairdo to the three-inch heels.

Julie practiced walking, looking over her shoulder at the mirror to check the effect.

On second thought, she might still have time to

change into her mid-calf-length blue knit dress.

Her buzzer sounded before she got to the closet.

Tom had climbed the stairs slowly, wondering if the barbaric rite of the bachelor party was worth his aching head and cottony mouth. The rented shoes squeaked and pinched his toes; he'd swear they weren't the ones he'd tried on a couple of weeks ago at the tux shop. On top of it all, he had to help jilted Julie land herself a man.

Think hoops, he told himself sourly. Nothing like a ball soaring through the air for a clean three-pointer. How hard could it be to give her a few pointers on attracting men? He'd been on the receiving end of some pretty potent techniques since adolescence.

He got to her door and took a deep breath, bracing himself for the worst. If she had trouble getting a date with a body like hers, it could be because she dressed like his ninety-year-old grandma. If that was the case, he'd be stuck with her until the reception was over. The only ones who'd be happy with that would be his matchmaking aunts.

This time she made him knock. He felt a small flicker of hope. She might have cold feet and back out.

Somewhere in the great urban sprawl of Chicago there had to be another pair of good Bulls tickets, and for the first time in years, he could afford to pay top dollar. He didn't have to go through with this charade for a chance to see some games. And suddenly he realized he didn't want to be responsible for Julie's love life.

The door slowly inched open, but he was unprepared for what he saw.

"There's nothing I can teach you about dressing to

kill,'' he said without thinking. ''You look gorgeous.''

''Thank you. It's nice of you to say so.''

''I wasn't trying to be nice. That dress is great.'' And so was the body poured into it. Suddenly his head wasn't the only thing throbbing. ''Can I have a glass of water and a couple of aspirins?''

''Is a substitute okay?''

''Fine, thanks.''

She put on her coat without any assistance from him, while he stood by the sink in her little kitchen and swallowed a couple of white tablets. Her navy wool coat had a belt on the back and a Black Watch plaid scarf was tucked under the collar—exactly what he'd expect her to wear: sensible but not eye-catching. The dress was something else. He gulped a second glass of water, hoping his sister wouldn't blame him because the man of the hour had wanted to party till dawn.

''Ready?'' he asked.

''I'm not sure. I mean, how can I meet other men when I'm supposed to be with you? Maybe you should go without me.''

A few minutes ago he'd wanted exactly that, now he wasn't so sure. She needed a bodyguard in that dress; the least he could do was try to steer her toward some decent guy.

''I thought we had a deal,'' he reminded her.

''Yes, but here, take the tickets.''

She handed him a plain white envelope, but he gave it back.

''I'll buy them, or I'll earn them. You can't just give them to me as a gift.''

''Why not? That's how I got them.''

"That was different. Leave them here and come to the wedding with me. We'll see how things work out, but I'm having a hard time believing you need advice from me."

"It seems pointless to go. How will your friends know I'm with you, but not *with you?*"

"I'll take care of it." He managed a weak grin, then waited as she disappeared to put the tickets away.

Whatever he'd been drinking last night had given him X-ray vision, because when she returned, he could still see her in the red dress, even with the coat buttoned up.

At the church a short while later, Tom took his position as an usher and left Julie on her own to kill time until the ceremony. She signed the guest book under the jaundiced eye of its busty blond keeper, made an unnecessary trip to the rest room, looked at Sunday school rooms through the windows of locked doors and pretended to read notices on the bulletin board.

Feeling more self-conscious with each passing minute, she started looking for the back exit, but Tom waylaid her and insisted on ushering her to one of the choice aisle seats just behind those reserved for relatives of the bride.

"Don't you want to take your coat off?" he asked softly. "I can hang it up for you."

"It's cold in here," she lied.

"Hiding your assets?" he teased, then hurried back to his ushering duties.

She sat red-faced, thinking of all the clever quips she could have made.

Guests began arriving in droves, and the perfumed air around her seemed to get hotter as the rows filled. She unbuttoned her coat, then slipped her arms out, but kept it around her shoulders. She couldn't bring herself to sit there baring a shoulder; she wasn't cut out to be a bad girl. She was only staying because leaving would be too conspicuous—and her mentor was blocking the exit. He seemed determined to earn the Bulls tickets—even if she'd changed her mind.

The processional began at last. A little flower girl in a pale peach dress and bonnet conscientiously dropped white rose petals, followed by a bevy of bridesmaids in high-waisted, narrow-skirted, moss-green velvet gowns. Julie had to give the bride high marks on her choice of dresses, but she dreaded the reception even more now. She'd never seen so many slender, gorgeous bridesmaids in one wedding. Her red dress was going to stand out like a zit among all those elegant attendants.

Everyone stood for the arrival of the bride, but Julie forgot her curiosity about Tom's twin. It suddenly hit her like a fist in the solar plexus: the woman was wearing her dress.

She'd gone to a dozen shops to find the perfect bridal gown, and she should be wearing it and coming down the aisle on her father's arm. She closed her eyes, suddenly hating the idea of a stranger in her gown, then opened them, telling herself it was cowardly not to watch.

It was perfect: not gaudy or overdone, but a dream of a dress with a delicately beaded satin bodice hugging the bride's breasts and waist and a skirt that floated along on the white carpet runner like a shimmering cloud.

Julie's eyes misted, and she forced herself to look at the bride's face, a feminine version of Tom's good looks. She was striking, not surprising since her twin brother was the sexiest man Julie had ever met. She must have been crazy—and a little desperate—to ask him for help. Whatever had made her think he'd want to play Henry Higgins to her Eliza Doolittle? When this was over—and it would be as soon as she could get a taxi and make her escape—she'd mail him the tickets with an apology for intruding on his sister's wedding.

The groom was handsome—no surprise—but he was either hungover from the bachelor party or scared to death. His face was pale and wan under waves of coal-black hair, but when he stepped forward and smiled at his bride, his features dramatically lit up.

Now that she thought about it, Brad had never looked at her that way. To her surprise and relief, she didn't much care anymore. Brad loved Brad. She'd had a narrow escape. She'd cast him in the role of her true love because she'd desperately wanted one special person in her life, but he'd blown it. *Him,* not her.

Coming to this wedding was shock treatment. Watching another woman get married in her dress was devastating, but it stirred up good, constructive anger. She was a nice person, and she hadn't deserved to be jilted.

She let the coat slide off her shoulders. No more sitting home feeling sorry for herself! She was going to find out if bad girls did have more fun.

After the newlyweds rushed down the aisle, beaming at each other, the two ushers remained at the front to dismiss the guests row by row. Tom was standing at her side, smiling and exchanging words with people as they got up to leave. Some men looked stiff and uncomfortable in tuxes, but Tom looked totally at ease in the black formal wear and stiff white shirt. His tousled dirty-blond hair curled over the collar of the jacket in back and spilled over his forehead, softening the thrust of high cheekbones and a strong chin. She was close enough now so she couldn't see his face without looking up, but the part of him at eye level gave her little shivers. His stomach was flat and his fine-tuned, muscular body put her imagination in overdrive.

"Your turn," he bent and whispered, his mouth so close to her ear she could feel a warm tickle of air. "I'm glad you took your coat off."

She pulled it on as she joined the crowd flowing down the aisle to a receiving line near the outer door. Shy about introducing herself to the bride wearing her dress, Julie found a deserted spot beside the guest book to wait for Tom.

"I see you're with Tom."

The well-endowed blonde who'd manned the book looked her over with a semihostile stare.

"Yes, I am."

Any urge she had to explain the tentative nature of their date vanished in the competitive glare coming from behind false eyelashes thick enough to double as pastry brushes.

So much for making new friends.

When Tom found her, he insisted she meet Tina, and the moment wasn't as awkward as Julie feared. Then she rode alone with him to the reception that was being held in a lodge hall rented for the occasion.

Thankfully, the trip was a short one, and they made a few conventional comments about the wedding that served as conversation.

Inside the large squat building, Tom led her to portable coatracks lining the entry hall and scanned the crowd through the double doors of the main room where a three-piece band was tuning up. She unbuttoned her coat, but he was behind her, helping her out of it, before she could do it herself. When he let his fingers brush against her bare shoulder, Julie tingled all the way to her tailbone.

"Tom, save a dance for me."

A tall, honey-haired bridesmaid wiggled her fingers at him as she passed.

"Terrific job, Brenda," Tom called over to her.

What job? Julie wanted to ask. All a bridesmaid had to do was glide down the aisle and stand there. She'd done the hesitation-two-step herself more times than she cared to remember.

The guest book girl cornered Tom as soon as they walked into the reception room.

"You look great in that tux, Tom."

"So did the fifty guys who wore it before me, Karla."

"I'll bet you can't wait to get out of it," she trilled.

"If I need any help with the studs, I'll let you know."

"Is she a bad girl?" Julie asked when the woman moved on to easier prey.

"She's…a lot of fun." He grinned wickedly and put his arm around Julie's waist. "Can I get you a drink? We're not supposed to start having fun until the happy couple has posed for enough photographs to paper their living room."

"A lemon-lime soda would be nice, thank you."

"Wrong! You should ask for a white wine spritzer or a gin and tonic, even if you intend to pour it in a planter when my back is turned."

"Even if I'm dying of thirst and gin makes my nose swell?"

"Your nose?" He examined her face with his sizzling brown eyes.

"Just kidding, Tom. I can handle a white wine if I have to. Do bad girls have to drink?"

"Nope, they don't have to do anything. That's the point. I'll go get the soda. In a plastic cup, who can tell?"

He joined a small crowd milling around the bar, leaving her alone. She looked around, wishing she knew someone. The bad-girl rules notwithstanding, a party was a lot more fun seen from a congenial cluster of female friends.

"Did I see you with Tom?" a man asked.

Tom was right. Alone worked better.

"Yes, but we're just friends." She'd thought that up ahead of time, in case he didn't get the word out to all the men at the reception.

"Then Tom's dumber than I thought. I'm Jerry."

"Jerry like Madonna, or do you have another name?"

She was on tonight. Too bad she felt like a fall guy for the Three Stooges.

"I'm glad you asked that. Actually, I'm proud of my family name, even though it's a little unusual. Poomph. Jerry Poomph. Rhymes with oomph. Would you like to dance?"

"There's no music yet."

"I make my own music, and I like to dance dirty."

"Goodbye, Poomph," Tom said, approaching him from behind.

"Just getting acquainted with your friend, Tom. She looks like fun."

"She's not."

"No problem. This is the mother lode—what with all those flight attendant friends of your sister's."

Poomph sauntered away, hands in his pockets to hike up his jacket and stretch the navy gabardine of his slacks tight across his butt. Even nice girls knew that old trick.

"You didn't need to play big brother," she told Tom, accepting a plastic cup from him. "I know how to get rid of men. My problem is finding a keeper."

"Remember the pointer I gave you earlier? Don't hang out with a jerk just because you don't like standing alone."

"I know what not to do," she said. "Tell me what I should do."

"Nothing."

His smile made a hidden heat source flare up; he should be penalized for hitting below the belt.

"Nothing? You keep telling me that. Next you'll tell me to be myself, and I can tell you how well that works."

"Will you dance with me if I take my shoes off?"

"Well, sure, I guess so."

"I hate rented shoes."

He slipped out of them and kicked them out of the way against the cement block wall behind him.

"We can't dance yet. The bride and groom aren't here," she said.

"Do you hear music?"

"Well, yes, they just started playing, but—"

"A bad girl has to be willing to break with tradition. Anyway, my sister will blame me, not you."

He led her to the empty center of the room, the hardwood floor waxed for dancing, and caught her up in his arms, then hesitated.

"Give me your shoes."

"I won't step on your toes. I'm a good dancer."

"Glad to hear it." He bent and lifted one of her feet, removing her shoe. Aware of a few curious glances, she quickly slipped out of the other, and he stuffed one in each of his jacket pockets.

"Now they'll know you're here," he said wickedly, beginning to dance, leading her as she'd never been led before.

His hand was low on her hip; his breath was warm on her forehead. They couldn't have danced more in sync if she'd been standing on top of his feet. She turned her head to the side, afraid of smearing lipstick on his gleaming white shirt, but he bent and pressed his cheek against hers. It was a tango position, but he managed to dance that way to the band's sentimental slow number.

No one joined them on the dance floor.

All they needed was an overhead floodlight to qualify as the featured attraction. When, finally, the band paused between numbers, she snatched back her shoes and literally ran off the floor.

She hid in the rest room for fifteen minutes and then came out, determined to show him she was a fast learner.

"See how you like me now, Dr. Frankenstein," she muttered under her breath.

It was easier than she'd dreamed possible. After the risqué dance with Tom, she didn't have to spend a moment alone. She ate dinner with a minor league baseball player who asked for her number afterward, and danced with so many men she started forgetting their names. But she didn't forget Peter Carlyle's. He was russet-haired and dimpled, easily the cutest of the groomsmen, and after their fourth dance, he stuck by her side.

Tom had been watching his protégé, not surprised by the attention she was getting, but not exactly thrilled by it, either. Not that he cared. She certainly wasn't his type, but he didn't want to be responsible for her hooking up with a loser. When dopey Pete Carlyle started climbing all over her on the dance floor, Tom knew it was time to cut in.

"How are things going?" he asked, looking down into Julie's eyes and wondering whether her cheeks were flushed from champagne or the overwhelming popularity he couldn't help observing. "I see you're wearing shoes."

"My feet got cold."

Her hand felt small in his, but the sway of her hip under his outstretched palm was anything but little-girlish. Either she was slightly tipsy or she learned fast—real fast. She melted against him, making him feel big, clumsy—and oh, so aroused.

He let his eyelids droop, but he was anything but sleepy. His mind was clicking through the guest list, sorting out the absolute jerks from the possibles. The sooner she hooked up with someone decent, the better for his libido. He had to remind himself that the red dress, champagne flush and sexy dance were only window dressing. She was looking for a lot more than a good time, and he wasn't on the candidate list, no matter how much he'd like to peel down her panties and teach her all there was to know about being a really bad girl.

"You don't need to worry about taking me home. Peter's going to," she said.

"Peter's been engaged four times."

"Oh, he told me all about it."

She wasn't a good liar. She wasn't the most seductive woman he'd danced with that evening, either, but she felt the best. Her firm, lush breasts were crushed against his chest, and the stiff shirt wasn't armor enough to keep him from imagining her nipples against his bare skin.

He was trying to put distance between them and still keep dancing—a technique he'd never tried to master—when she put both hands behind his neck and pulled his head down.

"Thanks for all you've done," she whispered.

The light whisper of her breath on his earlobe sent shock waves to his groin, but she immediately put space between them.

She was achingly appealing in her innocence, which was exactly why he preferred not-so-innocent girls. Women like Julie came with strings attached, and he wasn't ready for that.

He glanced over at his new brother-in-law, his friend since high school, and saw a clear mental picture of a ball and chain on the groom's ankle. Tom was happy for his sister, but her husband's nights out with the boys would be drastically curtailed from now on.

The song ended and Julie slipped away from him into Peter's unsuitable arms. Then the lights were turned down low for the last dance of the evening. Tom didn't have any trouble claiming Brenda Butler as his partner. She worked with Tina, but they'd just met. He'd singled her out at the rehearsal dinner as the bridesmaid most likely to....

Now this girl was sending him all the right signals. He was aching for a big score—at least a couple of home runs—and if he blew it now, who knew when he'd ever see her again. She was based out of Atlanta on international flights, the perfect scenario for some commitment-free good times.

"I'm really glad I finally met Tina's sexy brother," Brenda cooed.

Her pelvis grazed his groin, and he knew he was going to hate himself in the morning—not to mention most of the night.

"I came with someone," he reluctantly admitted. "She'll expect me to take her home."

"Oh, I'm so disappointed."

Her pout could get her arrested in half of the civilized world.

"I am, too, but you wouldn't think much of me if I dumped my date, would you?"

"I'd think you were terrible—for at least thirty seconds." She teased him with a laugh that made her vibrate under his touch.

He had a feeling she was a *very* bad girl.

The dance ended, and the lights went on, and the party was officially over. He found Julie, extricated her from Peter in spite of protests from both of them, and kept a firm hold on her arm while he worked their way through the departing guests to their coats.

"I don't know why you insist on taking me home. Peter was perfectly willing—"

"Peter is always willing. I don't know about the 'perfect' part. Anyway, you need a lot more lessons before you get into a car alone with a man who could sell snowblowers in Florida.''

"I'd be all right with Peter.''

"Maybe—if he were sober.'' Or better still, sedated.

"Do I get a diploma when I've finished my training? Or will you just present me with Mr. Right?''

He liked it when she was lippy. Meek, submissive women weren't for him—but neither was Julie Myers. He had to get outside and cool down quick—or go back to find Brenda.

He released her arm just long enough to grab both coats, then steered her to a spot by the wall.

"Taking me home isn't part of our deal!'' she insisted.

Her eyes sparkled with anger. He was in big trouble here.

"I brought you. I'll take you home. That's the way it works.''

"What works? We're not dating.''

"It's proper etiquette.''

It was a dumb thing to say, but she wouldn't believe the truth. He didn't have a clue why he'd blown off the bad-girl bridesmaid to take Julie home. It certainly wouldn't contribute anything to his peace of mind.

3

His car must have shrunk.

The restored '56 VW Beetle had seemed too small for Tom's broad shoulders and long legs on the way to the wedding, but now he filled it like an oyster in its shell. Julie kept her arms pressed to her sides to avoid brushing against him and her knees locked together so she wouldn't knock against his fingers clutching the gear knob.

Even if they weren't actually touching, he was getting inside her every time she inhaled his aftershave. Actually it was making her a little dizzy. Maybe he'd enhanced his own fragrance dancing cheek-to-cheek with the bridesmaid with the big teeth.

"You really didn't have to take me home." She was repeating herself, but what else was there to say to a man who'd spent most of the evening turning the fox-trot into foreplay?

"Just think of me as your designated driver."

"I carried around more champagne than I drank," she protested.

"I noticed. But Peter wasn't pouring his in the ice tub whenever he thought no one was watching."

"Just because we were having fun doesn't mean he was drunk."

He eased the car to a stop. "Here we are. I'll walk you to your door."

He had a real knack for dodging the subject.

"You don't need to. There's no place for an ax murderer to lurk between here and the door."

"Indulge me. Let me pretend I'm a gentleman."

"Is that what you're doing?" She hadn't intended to giggle, but it slipped out.

"Is it so far-fetched that I might have manners?"

"No, of course not." Another giggle. Darn, maybe she had had too much champagne.

She sat still as Tom got out and strode in front of the car to the passenger side. With a dark overcoat flapping around the satin-striped trousers, he could pass as an aristocratic playboy. Only his unruly hair didn't fit the image.

He walked her to the door with his ungloved hand on her waist, and she felt the heat of his fingers through her wool coat. Or thought she did. All her body parts were twitchy tonight. Remembering how her nose had itched from champagne bubbles, she struggled to resist rubbing it.

When she unzipped her purse to hunt for her key ring, he took the bag from her and reached inside, pulling out her keys and picking the one for the vestibule lock on the first try.

"How did you know which one to use?"

"Experience." He grinned wickedly, and she decided he'd just made a lucky guess.

"Well, thanks," she said.

"Portal to portal." He gestured for her to proceed him up the first flight of stairs. "The gentleman's code."

"Really, you're being..." She was going to say

"silly," but what was the point of debating with her escort—her paid escort.

Once she gave him the Bulls tickets, he'd disappear. She'd bribed him to show her how to put some sizzle into her life, and she'd had a great time after their attention-getting dance. She appreciated meeting Peter. He was cute, and unlike most men, he knew how to talk to a woman—no dopey come-ons or sports stories.

"I had a good time. Thanks," she said in front of her door, attributing her slight breathiness to the climb to the third floor. "If you'll wait just a minute, I'll give you the tickets."

He unlocked her door and handed her the keys.

"I haven't earned them yet," he said.

"You've already missed one of the games. I really want you to take them with you now, so no more will go to waste."

He'd feel like a jerk if he took her valuable tickets for doing practically nothing.

"At least let me pay for them." He followed her through the doorway; he didn't want to lurk in her hallway.

"No, we had a deal. I had a great time, but it was a silly idea—asking you to tutor me."

"You went to the head of the class tonight."

She was fun to tease, and she deserved to squirm a little, even if she didn't know it. Passing up a private party with Brenda was no small sacrifice, and he wasn't even sure why he'd done it.

"Then let the tickets be my way of thanking you."

Her cheeks were a glowing pink, either from the cold outside or the overheated air between them. She didn't have the wilted look a lot of really good-looking women got after an evening of partying. In fact, she'd even looked super under the harsh lights in the vestibule.

"Now what did I do with those tickets?" She frowned and looked around, as though they'd walked off. "They were in a white envelope. Let me think where I put them."

"There's really no rush...."

"No, let me think a minute."

"You were a little rattled about our date. It will come back to you."

"I certainly wasn't rattled! And it wasn't a date."

"I made that pretty clear at the reception. I let it be known—subtly, of course—that I wouldn't get mad if anyone else made moves on you."

"Subtly? The way you were dancing with...well, your moves are anything but subtle."

Brenda's motel phone number was burning a hole in his pocket, and he wondered again why he'd bothered to bring Julie home himself. He didn't want to feel responsible for her, and he certainly didn't want to be involved with a starry-eyed, would-be bride. Maybe Peter was her type, but he hoped she could do better. At least he'd given them both a cooling down period. It wouldn't be on his conscience if she made another bad choice.

"Talk about not being subtle, what about the dancing exhibition you and Carlyle put on?"

"It was just ordinary dancing. Maybe I put the tickets on my desk."

She started fumbling through a letter holder, then paused to step out of her heels.

"Sure, if someone'd put a piece of paper between

the two of you, it would have been mashed to a pulp,'' Tom said.

He was feeling decidedly cranky, and not just because Brenda would be flying out the following morning before they'd had a chance to get better acquainted.

In spite of her hard-luck history with men, Julie was dangerous. She was too damned adorable and sexy in that dress, and without heels she had a vulnerable, kittenish look that could drive a guy bonkers. If he had any sense, he'd forget the tickets and beat a hasty retreat.

His first instinct had been right: the sooner his ''pupil'' hooked up with someone else, the less tempted he'd be to ask her to a movie or something—just for companionship, of course. But serious girls like her were hopeless when it came to casual dating, and he didn't want to give her any false signals.

''You're someone to talk about dirty dancing! The way you held me…'' she sputtered.

''It was nothing like the stranglehold Pete used that last dance.''

''As if you weren't too busy to notice!''

''Not only did I notice, I can demonstrate the difference.''

He captured her hand and pulled her into the classic dance position.

''Notice my flawless style, my even-handed grasp, the current of air swirling between our bodies.''

He twirled her around, narrowly missing an end table, and led her into a deep dip.

''Our first dance was nothing like this!'' she protested, her soft, tinkling laughter giving him goose bumps.

"Peter is more of a hands-on dancer," he insisted. "Like this."

He pulled her closer, knee to knee, chest to breast, tickling his nose on the soft dark hair hugging the crown of her head.

"And no one could miss his hand action," he whispered close to her ear, letting his hand drop lower as they swayed without music in the small space in front of her couch.

"He didn't do that," she protested when his fingers found the fullness of her bottom. "Are you coming on to me?"

"Never ask a man that. It's a serious tactical mistake."

"Why?"

"Ruins his pacing. Makes him come up with a whole new technique on the spur of the moment. It's sudden death for potential relationships."

"You're making that up."

The hard tip of one rented shoe grazed her stockinged toe, and she stepped between his feet to save her own, leaning against him to get her balance.

"Sorry," he apologized.

Boy, was he sorry. He looked down at her perfect breasts crushed against his starched shirtfront and nearly made the drastic mistake of sliding his fingers down her neckline.

"Look, Julie, I was out of line about the dancing." He released her and stepped away. "I'm glad you had a good time with Peter. I'll go now."

"The tickets…"

"Not necessary…forget 'em."

"No, I insist. While you were demonstrating dance holds, I remembered what I did with them."

She scampered off to the small kitchen and came back with a triumphant grin.

"I stuck them on the fridge with my lobster magnet before we left so I wouldn't lose them!"

"Why a lobster?" She could learn a thing or two about flattering the male ego.

"It was that or a rubbery thing with the pharmacy phone number."

"Claws or pills. Not much choice."

He stared at the tickets she was thrusting in his direction, still reluctant to take them. It was like being paid for acting in his own self-interest. The fewer girls like Julie walking around the Windy City area unattached, the safer he was—not that he'd ever met anyone exactly like her.

Somehow she'd eased him toward the door; the woman had a real talent for getting rid of men.

"Well, it's been nice knowing you," she said, slipping the envelope into his coat pocket in one smooth movement.

"I haven't done enough to earn them."

In spite of his protests she refused to take them back.

He reached out to shake her hand—Bulls tickets called for some significant gesture—but somehow his lips zeroed in on the smooth skin above one dark, sleek eyebrow. His kiss grazed her flesh, and she gasped in surprise. If this was how a platonic kiss felt, he'd better stick to handshakes.

"Good night," she said in a firmer voice than he could muster.

"Night—and thanks a lot for the tickets."

"Brad will eat his heart out."

He didn't immediately remember who Brad was.

By the time he recalled her ex-fiancé, he'd raced down two flights of steps and stepped outside into a blanket of stinging wind-driven snow.

Julie watched him climb into the little blue Volkswagen, make a sharp circular turn, and putt away in the rear-engine vehicle.

Who would have guessed he'd turn sweet and kiss her? Or did it count as a kiss? Maybe it was more a lip press than the real thing.

Either way, her forehead tingled from the warm contact of his lips, and she felt branded where he'd playfully fondled her bottom, not very accurately imitating Peter's dance style.

She was out of her league and too drowsy to wonder why she felt like melting like the Wicked Witch of the West. If this was how bad girls felt, she was ready to join their ranks.

Tom woke up slowly and reluctantly the next morning, squinting against the bright winter sun streaming through half-closed blinds.

The phone penetrated his skull on its fourth shrill ring, but he wasn't going to answer it. He was supposed to be at his parents' house watching Tina rip open wedding presents, as though a pair of newlyweds had nothing better to do.

''Ridiculous,'' he said sullenly, glad he'd never be a bridegroom dragged from a honeymoon bed to rush over to the new in-laws, as if everyone in the room—his saintly mother included—wouldn't be wondering how the wedding night went.

He wasn't hungover, but he was dumbfounded. What the devil had he pulled last night, demonstrating dance techniques and kissing Julie's forehead? He hadn't done anything that dorky since he dropped a goldfish down the front of a girl's blouse in his junior high days.

The phone rang again, and he pushed away the covers, shivering as he padded buck naked to the phone on the kitchen counter. Instead of picking it up, he let the machine take it while he found a robe, then ran through his messages: a sultry goodbye from Brenda; an invitation to some friend's party from Karla—it took him a minute to remember who she was; Pete's voice asking for Julie's phone number.

"Damn," he said aloud.

Why hadn't the dope remembered to ask her for it himself? Hadn't he done enough, bringing her to the reception? He should let Pete stew awhile.

But he was going to call right away and get it over with. He wanted his friends to go for Julie. Quadruply engaged Peter was actually looking for Ms. Right, or he wouldn't keep getting engaged. And the sooner Julie Myers was safely out of circulation, the better for his peace of mind. Putting his lips anywhere on her was a very bad move; she was just too darn kissable—too darn lovable—for any bachelor's safety.

He wasn't one to kid himself. She was a looker, funny and sweet, too. He certainly wouldn't mind taking her to bed—right now would do nicely—but he was only interested in Ms. Right Now, not Ms. Right.

Unfortunately, she needed a few more pointers, and he still felt obligated to do more to earn the Bulls tickets. But as soon as one of his buddies took the bait, he could dissociate himself from her.

"Dissociate." He tested the word aloud, and it had a good ring.

As long as he kept a businesslike perspective, he wouldn't fall into Julie's trap himself.

In spite of his good intentions, he didn't get around to phoning Julie with more good advice that day—or the next, or the next.

On Wednesday morning he sold a three-part entertainment center he'd been hoping to unload for months. He wouldn't make the mistake of stocking another. Finishing something that large intimidated his customers. They wanted quick weekend projects like a chest of drawers or a rocking chair, and he didn't blame them. Why commit all that time and effort to something that might not be satisfactory when it was done?

Why make a long-term commitment to one woman when it meant giving up a rich and varied social life?

Where had that thought come from?

He took the afternoon off, letting his assistant handle the sluggish midwinter business, and spent ninety minutes working out at the gym. He made it a point not to wonder whether Julie Myers had heard from Peter or any of the other guys who'd been sniffing around her at the reception.

Back at his apartment, he checked his messages. Only one caught his attention.

"Hi, Tom. Remember me? Brenda. You're probably surprised to hear from me again so soon, but my schedule got changed. I'm flying out of O'Hare for Rome tomorrow. And guess what? I'm available to-night—all night. I'd love to see you."

So now maybe he had a dinner date, but did she plan to use his place for the overnight layover? She hadn't left a phone number—an ominous sign. He was debating whether to do some serious cleaning, but only got as far as tossing out the milk carton he'd emptied on his cereal that morning when the phone rang.

"So, Tom, did you get my message?" Brenda purred with all the subtlety of the star of a triple-X video.

"Yeah. How about Chinese for dinner?" he asked.

"Wonderful! I'm in the mood for something exotic, spicy—"

"Where can I pick you up?"

"I'm at the Homecrest Motel on Hagenback Road."

"I know the place. Give me an hour."

"I plan to give you more than that."

He dropped the phone with a klunk. Talk about easy. Brenda certainly took the challenge out of the chase. In fact, he was more in the mood for some good conversation and an action-packed special-effects movie than he was for playing superstud. One thing he'd forgotten to tell Julie: the bad-girl game took a lot of stamina.

The Bulls tickets were still on his black-enameled, gold-trimmed dresser—a piece he'd finished himself to display when the store first opened. He couldn't sign off on Julie yet—not after accepting what turned out to be great seats. There were still a few things he could teach her. In fact, he'd been really derelict in that duty.

The wedding gown ad was still lying by the phone. He punched in her number, then checked the clock on the stove. He'd have to hustle to pick up his apartment, shower and meet Brenda in anything like an hour.

"Hello. We're not available right now, but please leave your name and number so we can get back to you."

Tom hung up, smiling at Julie's roommate pretense. Not that he blamed a single woman for letting a caller think she didn't live alone. But it could be off-putting to a guy calling for a date, not knowing if she lived with a girl or a guy. She still had a lot to learn.

He didn't think leaving a message on her machine would do justice to the next installment of the bad-girl rules.

When he got to the motel, Brenda was ready, but not to go out in the blustery near-zero weather.

"I thought we'd eat early and take in a movie," he suggested, immediately noticing she was braless under a short, form-hugging, lime-green dress. He didn't remember her mouth being that large, but maybe it was a good thing. She seemed to have more teeth than most people.

"Or we could order in." She moistened her lower lip with her tongue.

He'd have to mention that technique to Julie—and caution her not to use it unless she was issuing an invitation.

"You deserve better than cardboard-flavored Chinese. I know a place that serves authentic Cantonese."

By some odd coincidence it was only a few blocks from the flower shop where Julie worked. One quick stop and he could indulge in sweet-and-sour with a clear conscience. He hustled Brenda out to the car.

"I need to make a stop," he said as he pulled into

the parking area by the flower shop just in time to avoid being locked out of the business. "Wait here— I'll only be a minute."

"Tommy, you don't need flowers to make me blossom."

He left the motor running, not that the heater in the VW could deliver much warmth. He couldn't believe he was letting a gorgeous, available woman cool off in his tin igloo while he went to dish out more advice to Julie. He was eager to see her safely out of circulation, but maybe this was going too far.

Julie liked her job too well to be a clock watcher, but she was glad it was nearly closing time. The drive home on dark winter evenings was lonely, especially after the fun she'd had at the wedding. Not that anything had come from her fling as a bad girl. There were cobwebs on her phone.

She finished polishing the doors of the refrigerated case and carried her supplies to the back room, intending to come right back and flip the Closed sign on the door—no reason not to lock up a few minutes early—when the chimes on the door alerted her to the arrival of a last-minute customer.

Millie, the owner, was already preparing the deposit in her office, so Julie hurried to greet the new arrival—and froze halfway to the counter.

"Tom." Her heart skipped a beat—a wholly involuntary reaction to his rugged good looks and aggressively masculine body in tight jeans and bomber jacket—but she forced herself to be cool. "Can I help you with something?"

"I just wanted to talk to you."

"Well, I am working."

She couldn't imagine what he wanted to say, but whatever it was, she didn't want him to know how much she'd thought about him since he'd said good-bye with a kiss on her forehead.

"So make a little bouquet for me."

"A bouquet of what?"

"You choose. You know, something nice. No carnations dyed blue."

She walked over to the case, feeling his eyes on her even though she was shapeless in one of the full pink smocks Millie provided for all her employees.

"Maybe pink and white ones?" she suggested, peering into the case as though she didn't know the stock down to the last little bud.

"Fine."

He was so indifferent she felt guilty suggesting anything but the cheapest possible arrangement.

"I wanted to warn you," he said, "Peter asked me for your number. Has he called yet?"

"No. Do you want baby's breath?"

"Whatever you think. If he hasn't called yet—"

"There's no reason to think he will," she said defensively.

"He will—and he probably won't be the only one. But you'll get off to a bad start if you accept a date for Saturday this late in the week."

The door tinkled again, but Julie was too rattled to notice who came in.

"You don't have to coach me anymore." She spun around and held up the rather meager bouquet for his approval. "Pink or red ribbon?"

"Yes, I do. Either. Now listen, whatever you do, don't let a guy think you're available on short notice.

Make him worry a little so he'll put himself out to ask early next time.''

"For me?" A leggy, big-toothed woman walked over and linked arms with Tom.

Julie didn't know if the bridesmaid recognized her in the demure pale smock, but Brenda's perfume alone was enough to make her as memorable as a case of poison ivy.

Julie walked over to wrap the flowers in a cone of green tissue, making out a bill and processing Tom's credit card without looking up at him.

"Don't forget what I told you," he warned in a low voice, thrusting the flowers at Brenda and turning to leave.

"Well, Mr. Expert," Julie said when the door closed behind them, "how much advance notice did you give Brenda, the bad bridesmaid?"

4

That night Julie made a pact with herself: Wednesday phone call, yes to a date; Thursday, no.

Why did it feel as if she'd made a deal with the devil?

She wasn't even sure she liked Brunswick, so why on earth was she listening to his advice? An even better question was, Why had he interrupted his date with the bridesmaid to insist Julie play hard to get?

She should have sold him the basketball tickets. Then he wouldn't feel obligated to help her, and she wouldn't be pushing bits of warmed-over, made-from-a-box macaroni and cheese around on her plate, her appetite ruined by unwelcome speculation about Tom doing the horizontal bop with Brenda.

"Maybe they went to a movie," she suggested out loud, dumping most of her dinner into the garbage.

What difference did it make to her anyway? It was one thing to imagine his long, muscular legs entwined with hers, his firm lips tasting the honey of her skin, and quite another to risk losing her heart to a hunk whose taste in women was definitely in Brad's class. For every good, reliable man, there seemed to be a hundred who thought a stripper was a sex goddess.

She couldn't beat 'em, so she'd better join 'em. Her success at the reception proved men were attracted to girls who made their own rules: bad-girl rules. But she didn't need lessons to turn her life around, only nerve, and she was mad enough to try anything. Mad at Brad for being such a jerk, and mad at Tom for having rotten taste in women.

Not that it mattered to her.

The phone rang, and her first thought was that Tom had dumped Big Tooth. Then she wanted to bang her head against the wall for having such a dumb reaction.

She grabbed the phone, welcoming any call to jolt her back to reality.

"Hello, is this Julie Myers?" an unfamiliar voice asked.

"Yes," she admitted guardedly, thinking of the quickest way to get rid of telemarketers. Saying she'd just lost her job was getting stale.

"This is Jerry."

"Jerry?" She drew a blank.

"Jerry Poomph, rhymes with oomph. We chatted at the wedding."

"Oh, sure. Hi, Jerry."

"How ya doing?"

"Great, just great."

"I thought maybe I'd put a little oomph in your life, say Saturday night."

Wednesday, yes; Thursday, no. But it wasn't a pact signed in blood.

"I'm sorry, Jerry. It's really nice of you to ask, but I have other plans."

"What other plans?"

"A date." Too vague. "A date with an old friend."

"Male or female?"

"Male." Snoop!

"Where are you going?"

"Well, we haven't exactly decided yet."

"I'm a night owl. How about you and I go out after he drops you off?"

"No, that's not a good idea."

"You don't know what you're missing, sweetie."

"I have a pretty good idea. Goodbye, Jerry."

She didn't need that much of a reality jolt!

Heavy wet snow blanketed the city the next day, and Julie could have gotten home from work quicker by pushing her car. She gritted her teeth at the traffic tie-ups, uncommonly eager to get home from the flower shop. There had been a rush on bouquets of pink carnations, or so it seemed, and every one she handled made her wonder what Brenda had done with Tom's indifferent offering. Was the woman imaginative enough to scatter petals on the sheets, or was she the sentimental type, pressing one as a love token in a scrapbook? Julie couldn't see her doing either—not that it was any concern of hers.

When she finally got home, her mother called and talked endlessly about a friend who was divorcing after thirty-seven years of marriage.

"I just can't understand it," her mother said for the twentieth time. "Why now after so many years together?"

"Mom, what I know about true love could get lost in a flea's pocket."

"Dear, I don't think fleas have pockets."

"You're probably right. Talk to you later, Mom."

Her mother took things so literally, the woman practically saluted her husband. When she swore to obey in her wedding vows, she meant *OBEY*.

Julie momentarily wondered if she'd been switched at birth, but that fruitless line of speculation was interrupted by another call.

"Julie, this is Peter Carlyle."

"Oh, hi. It's good to hear from you, Peter." She smiled into the phone until she remembered it was Thursday.

"I was hoping maybe we could get together Saturday evening."

"Saturday…Saturday…I'd love to…"

Thursday is too late, a bossy male voice in her head insisted.

"But I'm afraid I have other plans," she said.

"Oh, that's too bad."

He sounded so sad, she wished she could pat him on the head and console him.

"I'm really sorry," she said in her most soothing voice, not sure how well Peter handled rejection.

"I'll just have to call earlier next time," he said cheerfully enough, obviously not mortally wounded.

That was silly, she thought after she hung up. She'd turned down an evening with a nice guy on the basis of what was probably bad advice.

She made her own plans for Saturday night, but when it arrived, she didn't feel up to trying a new hair conditioner or cleaning the lime deposits off the shower tiles.

Was she like her mother, bowing to the voice of authority just because it was a deep sexy bass?

No way! She wasn't letting a virtual stranger mastermind her love life—or what passed as one. She was only sitting home alone on a Saturday night because—well, because there was a certain satisfaction in lounging around in sweatpants with her hair in a ponytail, anticipating a good, meaningless cry from the tear-jerking movie waiting to go into the VCR. And if she needed further compensation for turning down an evening of fun with a nice guy, there was a pint of chocolate fudge ripple in the freezer.

"I'm not home because Tom advised me," she told her violets as she watered the delicate little blooms struggling for life on her kitchen table. "It makes good sense not to be overly eager."

Being on twenty-four-hour call whenever Brad wanted to see her had probably been a major blunder, much as it hurt to admit it now. She was only following her own good instincts by letting Peter know she wasn't available on short notice.

So why did she feel silly sitting home when she could be out having a good time?

The movie was melodramatic and dated, but she watched it to the weepy conclusion. Unfortunately it was only nine-thirty when it ended, too early for bed and too late to do the tiles.

She wasn't expecting company, so the door buzzer startled her, making her wonder whether to ignore it or answer.

Curiosity won out.

"Who is it?"

"Tom Brunswick. Can I come up?"

She took so long answering, Tom expected her to send him packing.

"Well, yeah, I guess so."

"Thanks a lot," he said under his breath. The woman had a genius for sending get-lost signals.

At least she'd followed his advice. Another buddy had let it be known how unhappy Peter was at being turned down. Was Julie unhappy, too?

This business of giving advice to the lovelorn had its downside. He'd dropped off a hot little number in skintight jeans she was willing to peel off just so he could check on Julie.

The quicker he put her out of his mind, the better. He'd sent Brenda and her bouquet packing after a quick bite to eat, much to his later regret. His sister's friend had been playing footsie fast and furious under the table, and while one part of his anatomy had definitely been paying attention, he hadn't been able to get Julie and her little pink smock out of his mind. She'd been unhappy with his advice, but she was a lamb among wolves when it came to managing her love life. How was she going to meet the right guy if she couldn't even handle the first-date stall?

If he had to curtail his own social life to put all his energy into pairing Julie with Mr. Right, it'd be worth it in the long run. Bulls tickets aside, he wanted her safely out of circulation—and, he had to admit, happy. Then he could get back to being footloose and fancy-free.

"What on earth are you doing here?" she asked from the doorway before he could catch his breath from running up the stairs.

"Just dropping in."

"Yes, but why?"

He wondered himself. At least she stepped aside and let him into her apartment.

"I was on my way home," he said by way of explanation. She didn't need to know he'd come thirty minutes out of his way after dropping off a hot date.

"Surely you had a date on Saturday night?"

"Just for dinner."

"You struck out?"

"No! I mean, you must have a pretty bad opinion of me. I live alone, but I don't like to eat alone, especially if I have to cook."

"Did you and the bridesmaid enjoy your dinner?"

"We had Chinese." He didn't want to talk about Brenda. She was probably blackening his name with flight attendants from here to Hong Kong.

"Egg rolls, fortune cookies?" Julie asked.

"The whole works—then I wished her a nice trip to Rome."

And she'd expressed a parting sentiment that had something to do with part of him shriveling up and falling off.

Julie looked considerably happier, but he didn't flatter himself that she was jealous. Nice girls like her just naturally disliked the Brendas of the world. He was glad he'd come to check on her. He hadn't looked twice at a girl with a ponytail since puberty, but Julie looked cute—even in a pair of sweats baggy enough for both of them to wear at the same time.

"Now tell me the truth. Why drop in on me?" she insisted.

"You did ask for my help."

"I've changed my mind."

"It's too late. If you want to find a keeper, you need all the help you can get."

"I don't know what's helpful about convincing me to sit home on a Saturday night."

He had a sneaky suspicion she was baiting him. He suspected she had a wicked sense of humor, but she'd met her match if she thought he was easily put off.

"I'm not sure being Peter's fifth fiancée will put you in the winner's circle. I'm sorry if I spoiled your fun, but you have to look at the big picture."

"You're making a single date sound like a military operation."

She grinned, and he was glad he'd come—solely to check on his pupil, of course.

"Hey, you asked me to help, and I'm no quitter. Step one is getting you into circulation. Step two is narrowing down the field. Then you can zero in on the right guy."

"And you're going to mastermind the whole process just to pay me back for the tickets?"

"That, too, but I like a challenge."

"Thanks a lot. Maybe you should branch out, get me in the personals or on the Net or in a magazine for mail-order brides."

"I didn't mean it that way. Attracting men isn't your problem—picking the best one is."

"If you say one word about Brad—"

"He's history." He held out his hands in a gesture of surrender and was relieved when she stopped scowling. "Let me make it up to you for staying home. Let's go out for pizza, and I'll give you a few more pointers about next week's dates."

"Assuming I'll have even one."

"With me as your consultant, you'll need a date book to keep them straight. Are we on for pizza?"

"Oh, sure, why not? Just give me a minute to change."

He started to say she was fine just the way she was, but who was he to come between a woman and her wardrobe? She'd done just fine dressing for the wedding, and he wasn't averse to seeing a few more curves than the sweats revealed.

She strolled casually to her bedroom, closed the door, and shimmied out of her baggy clean-the-bathroom sweats in the time it took for one deep breath. She was going for the Fastest Clothes Change world record.

Her second-best jeans had that casual prewashed look. She dove into them and grabbed a loose-fitting, dark wine sweater, pulling it over her head in seconds. The important thing to remember was that this wasn't a date, and primping of any kind was strictly uncalled for. She brushed the end of her ponytail, but didn't worry about a stray lock tickling her left cheek. Changing her hairstyle would send entirely the wrong message.

No self-respecting bad girl would dream of accepting a date from a drop-in. Going out for pizza with Tom was definitely not a date, and she couldn't make it seem like one by fussing over her appearance.

She allowed herself a dab of lipstick, but still worried he might misinterpret her clothes change as preparation for a date. She nearly switched back, but then time would be against her. Quick was casual; quick was imperative.

If Tom were the least little bit interested in her, he wouldn't be trying so hard to fix her up with someone else. And, of course, she couldn't allow herself to be interested in his type. She was ready to settle for one special man. And Tom had clearly expressed that it wasn't him. If he wanted variety in his life, it was fine with her.

Tom paced back and forth across the small, cozy living room, already regretting his off-the-cuff invitation. Naturally she had to change. Women had specific outfits for each and every activity in their lives. A female couldn't leave home wearing a watch-TV outfit. It would be a serious faux pas, like a guy going out with his zipper open.

Naturally she didn't realize that the male imagination kicked into overdrive as soon as a woman put a closed door between her and a man with the intention of removing clothing. He didn't want to think about her undressing just a few feet away, but that was the way a guy's mind worked. He couldn't help speculating how she looked in panties and bra, wondering if she wore chaste white cotton or sexy see-through lace.

Now that the closed door had triggered his X-rated vision, could he help it if he wondered how it would feel to creep up behind her and cup her breasts, then trail his fingers over her flat little belly and under the elastic of her panties.

He groaned.

"Are you all right?" she asked from behind the door.

Ohmigosh…he hadn't realized he'd actually groaned out loud.

"Just banged my shin on the table," he answered, quickly sitting and crossing his legs to conceal any contrary evidence, not that he felt guilty for letting his perfectly normal, fertile imagination lead him astray.

He must have been crazy to think he needed to come over to Julie's to check up on her. What had made him think she might be sprawled out on her couch doing some intense lip-locking with Peter—or one of his more dangerous buddies?

Idiot, he silently chided himself. Now you know she's not playing kissy-face with one of your friends—not yet anyway.

Sure, his ultimate goal was to see her safely settled with one guy—and she would be if she followed his advice—but there were a lot of pitfalls for a girl as vulnerable as Julie. He trusted her, but he knew the score. No guy started something with a woman in the hope of earning a ball and chain. Not ones he knew, anyway, and certainly not him.

A moment later she came out of the bedroom wearing faded jeans and a bulky sweater. He couldn't have made a better selection for her. True, the denim hugged her thighs and butt in a pretty eye-catching way, but he wouldn't be tempted to stare at her breasts when he sat across the table from her.

She put on a waist-length ski jacket with no help from him, and they were on their way.

His shop was in Roseville, so he knew this suburb pretty well even though he lived a ways away in South Barrett. The best pizza place around was only five minutes from her apartment, and she went along with his choice.

They didn't have much to say to each other. He heard her teeth chattering and knew how cold the VW seats were with only thin denim between the upholstery and her bottom.

He'd done it himself this time—triggered thoughts of her anatomy, warming himself with thoughts of her sleek, shapely behind.

"Sorry the car's so cold," he said. "I've got the van in the shop."

"Oh, it's okay."

He heard the light clicking of her teeth and ran a few yellow lights to get to their destination fast.

Armando's Pizza Palace was pleasingly gaudy with a ceiling of colored Christmas lights that stayed there permanently and pseudo-Roman columns that divided the sections of booths and tables. At this hour they snagged a choice booth in the rear, far away from a group of rowdy teenagers trying to impress their dates, and a family with fussy kids who should have been in bed.

"How do you like your pizza?" he asked.

She wiggled out of her jacket without making a

production of it and didn't bother looking at the menu. "Sausage, mushrooms and green peppers."

"I like the works. We'll get half and half. My secret vice is root beer. I've loved it since I was a kid. They frost the mugs here."

"That's a vice I can share. I haven't had root beer in ages."

When he'd suggested going for pizza, he'd forgotten how long it could take between ordering and actually getting the food. They would simply have to pass the time with more instruction.

"I feel bad about nixing your date with Peter, but—"

"I'll thank you later?"

She had a way of looking directly into his eyes, no lash-batting or coyness. She didn't use little feminine tricks like wrinkling her nose, tweaking her earlobe, running her finger from her chin down her throat, using gestures to call attention to her pretty face. He was trying to talk to her like a buddy, but he was the one fidgeting.

"Believe me, you haven't discouraged Peter," he said. "You only laid a few ground rules."

"I was annoyed at first, but you're probably right. I let Brad call all the shots—just the way my father does. He's ex-army, retired major. It shows."

"What does he do now?"

"Insurance. Believe it or not, my mother has never had a full-time job. She plays bridge. How about your parents?"

"Dad's a fireman. Mom helps me out at the shop now, but she used to run a day-care center. She came from a big family and wanted six kids of her own, but after Tina and me, she couldn't have more. Now she's ballistic about grandkids. I'm hoping Tina will take the pressure off me.''

''My brother Dean has two kids, but I don't think grandmothers are ever satisfied.''

''Why should they be? They play with good kids and send bad ones home to their parents.''

''You sound cynical.''

''Maybe.'' He grinned, ready to change the subject. ''So what do you do for recreation, Julie?''

He found out she had girlfriends; that was good. She liked sports—even better. By the time the pizza arrived, he'd determined that no serious character flaws would hinder her race to the altar. And the sooner she graduated from his school for husband-hunters, the happier he'd be. She had him between a rock and a hard place. Other women still turned him on, but thinking about Julie's problem seriously distracted him.

Normally, being with one woman and thinking about another wasn't bad, but even though Julie did have quite a body, her marriage-minded attitude had gotten under his skin. She was off-limits, but his libido was having a hard time remembering it.

The pizza had come hot from the oven, and trailed gooey cheese when he served a first piece to both of them.

''You're going to eat pizza with a fork?'' he teased.

''Just the first few bites—until it cools off and the cheese stops dripping.''

Her tongue caught a string of pale mozzarella and

she sort of twirled it into her mouth. He watched, fascinated, and forgot for a minute to bite into his own.

"It's sizzling," she gasped, "but delicious. I love things hot."

A bit of sauce was clinging to her upper lip where it formed a little bow. Without thinking, he reached across the table and blotted it on his napkin.

"Oh, wow, you must think I'm a sloppy eater! Is there some rule I'm breaking here?"

"None whatsoever."

He had no intention of telling her how sexy it was to watch her eat. She had a natural gift for approaching food in an erotic way. He wasn't going to say anything to make her self-conscious about it. Brad, the dud fiancé, must be an egomaniac to think he could do better than Julie—or maybe he just got cold feet when it came to making the big march down the aisle. Tom couldn't judge any guy too harshly for panicking when faced with the big "M." It scared him to death, too.

She couldn't believe she'd eaten half a pizza. Tom kept encouraging her, and she went hog-wild—with the emphasis on hog. Her waistband was tight, and eating late at night made her sleepy.

The cold air outside—and in the VW—revived her, but not enough to come up with a clever ploy for going up to her apartment unescorted. Not that she tried very hard. Even if this wasn't a date, she'd enjoyed herself—too much for her peace of mind.

"Well, would you like to come in for ice cream?" she asked outside her door.

"Okay."

"Actually, all I have is chocolate fudge ripple ice milk—lots of sugar but no fat, if that matters."

Apparently it didn't. He followed her in, and she had second thoughts. She didn't want him to think she was treating him like a date, especially after he refused to let her pay for half the pizza. She was only being polite; how could she know he'd accept?

Even before she snapped on the overhead light, she saw her message light blinking fast and furious. She wanted to ignore it, but Tom would probably think she was odd if she did. Anyway, it was probably her mom, or maybe Karen reporting on her first date with a new guy.

"Guess I'd better check it," she said somewhat apologetically as she pushed the play button.

"Hi, Julie. It's Peter. I know this is wild, and I'm not calling to check on you. Maybe I'm way out of line, but I didn't want to go out with anyone but you tonight. So, if you're not doing anything next Saturday, will you pencil me in, and I'll get back to you soon. 'Bye-bye.''

"I guess you believe me now," Tom said in a tone that could only pass as sarcastic.

"What do you mean?" She pressed rewind and watched until the machine was reset.

"Being a little standoffish at first pays off. Of course, maybe it's not a good thing to commit yourself this far in advance."

"You can't have it both ways, Brunswick! First

you thought Peter called too late. Now you think he called too early.''

''Or maybe he took his date home early and is doing a number on you, checking to see if you really went out.''

''You're impossible! I think it was a sweet gesture for him to call tonight. How can you find fault with Peter for asking me out a week in advance?''

''I'm not finding fault. You know, though, I'm really too full for ice cream.''

''Ice milk.''

''Whatever. I think I'll be going now.''

He'd just used her least favorite word in the world: whatever. It was such an offhand way to respond.

''I think you're annoyed because he called early.''

''No, but I think you've had enough tutoring for one night.''

''I have. Thanks for the pizza.''

He left before she could walk to the door with him. She pouted for a minute, then found cause for mild satisfaction. Tom's advice had paid off, but maybe not in the way he'd hoped.

What was Brunswick's game, and why did she care so much what he thought?

5

She couldn't believe it was already Thursday.

Happily, the days had flown by, because she was really looking forward to the weekend. Peter had come through in a rush of enthusiasm. He'd called on Monday and Wednesday evenings to confirm the details of their date.

Not only that, but she was going to have her first-ever Sunday brunch date with another guy who'd danced with her at the wedding: Alan Raynes. She only remembered him as a pair of broad shoulders and peppermint breath, but her drab, nonexistent social life had suddenly become an adventure.

She didn't even mind the forty-five minutes it took three thrifty octogenarians to select a funeral arrangement and divide the cost between them, although she did catch herself tapping her fingers while they decided which one would pay twenty-two odd cents instead of twenty-three.

She'd locked the shop door and put the Closed sign in place when one last die-hard customer knocked insistently on the window. Her boss didn't want her to open the door for latecomers, but she always felt self-conscious being visible in the well-lit interior as she did the closing chores. The least she could do was point to the sign and mouth that they were closed.

When she saw who was banging, she broke the rule and opened the door.

"Tom."

"Hi." He brought cold February air into the shop with him.

"If you need another bouquet, you'll have to buy one that's made up. I'm not supposed to let customers in after closing time."

"You're breaking a rule by letting me in?" He grinned broadly. "That's good. Makes a guy feel special."

"I'd make an exception for anyone I know."

"You're too honest."

"You make it sound like a character defect." A little laugh slipped out, but it was more a hiccup than good humor. "If you aren't buying flowers for your woman-of-the-night, why are you here?"

"Honest and brutally direct! Do you know what a lethal combination like that does to a girl's love life?"

"I have a pretty good idea," she said dryly, "but I guess I have to thank you for my return to the land of the dating."

"Peter called to set it up?" He didn't sound enthusiastic.

"Twice. Monday and last night."

"He's a little overeager."

"Thanks to your advice. I've never been unavailable for a date just because it was late in the week. My reward is two dates this weekend."

"Two? You accepted a second date with Peter before you went on a first one?" Now he sounded downright testy.

"Give me some credit! I'm going out with another friend of yours on Sunday—Alan Raynes."

"Raynes." He frowned, compressing his lips and drawing his brows together. His expression gave her a little shiver; she wouldn't want him to be really mad at her. "He's not a friend of mine."

"Well, he was at the wedding. He kept a peppermint candy in his cheek."

"Oh, yeah. He works with Dan, my brother-in-law. I guess he's okay."

"I'm only supposed to go out with guys on your approved list?" She didn't try to hide her annoyance. "Or do I have your permission to branch out?"

"Branch away. Do you meet a lot of guys here?" His gesture took in the whole interior of the shop crowded with everything from empty baskets to imported ceramics and silk arrangements.

"Lots." Most of them buying flowers for other women.

"This where you met Brad?"

Now he was getting down and dirty.

"No, he was a friend of a friend," she said in the haughtiest tone she could muster.

"I'm out of line on that subject, right?" His grin was catnip to a kitten, compelling her to smile in return.

"Way out. But I guess I owe you."

"For all my good advice?"

"No, for taking me to the wedding."

"Speaking of advice…"

"I don't remember mentioning it." Two could play his game.

"But you do remember asking for it?"

Just as in the corny old movies with sword fighting

that she loved, Brunswick certainly knew how to get inside her guard: parry, thrust and wound.

"Yeah, I asked for it."

"So when can we get together for another tutoring session?"

"You already know I'm busy Saturday and Sunday."

Wednesday, yes; Thursday, no. He'd warned her not to be too available; now she'd see how he liked it—not that he was asking for a date!

"How about tomorrow night, then?" he asked.

"No, tomorrow won't work. It's girls' night out."

"Can't you cancel? You can see your girlfriends anytime."

"We do something once a month, regardless. I've been friends with this group since junior high, and the rule is carved in stone: we get together, better offer or not."

"So my offer is better?"

He thought he had her.

"A lecture on dating etiquette? I don't think so!"

"Back in your school days, didn't you ever notice the bad girls were getting better offers and taking them? What do you do that's so much fun?"

"We go out for dinner, then to singles' night at the Bowl-O-Rama unless there's some special event."

"If you're like my sister and her friends, you probably spend most of the time talking about men."

"It's about bonding with friends, not dissecting men." She shouldn't have opened the door.

"You're cute when you pout." He ran one cold finger under her chin, this time giving her real shivers. "Back to the subject. Doesn't it make you a little wary when a guy calls for a Saturday night date on the Saturday night before?''

"I thought it was clever."

"Clever." He puckered his lips and expressed disapproval with a sour expression.

"You warned me against accepting a date if the guy calls too late. Now you want me to be suspicious because he calls too early. I thought bad girls made their own rules!''

"If you really want to be a bad girl, you'll blow off your girlfriends."

"For a last-minute offer? Sheesh! You're making me crazy!''

She looked down and found she'd just unrolled about a hundred feet of the lavender ribbon she'd been carrying.

"I don't want you to ditch your women friends to go out on a date. I just think you need some pointers before your love life gets too complicated."

"I've been on first dates before. I can handle them.''

He couldn't have looked more skeptical if she'd claimed to be dating an alien.

"All right," she conceded none too graciously, giving up on the ribbon and sticking the roll under the counter to rewind in the morning. "You're right. I asked for your help."

"Paid for it, actually. I'm looking forward to my first game next week."

"So I need your advice. Why not tonight?''

She took his hesitation as an answer. She had a funny little pain in her chest as she wondered what the flavor of the week was: blonde, brunette or redhead.

She visibly drooped, and he felt mean-spirited, as if he'd just stolen a little girl's doll. He resented being the heavy; she was the one with the full social calendar.

"I guess we'll just have to skip it," she said, feigning a matter-of-fact tone but not fooling him.

He hadn't intended to tell her where he was going that evening, not that it was any big deal. He just didn't want to feel obligated to invite her along. For some reason, whenever he was around her, his mouth engaged itself before his brain kicked in.

"No, this is a crucial point in your lesson. I guess you could come along." He'd done it again.

"Where?"

Did he only imagine the sudden sparkle in her deep blue eyes?

"My aunt Betty's. You may remember her from the wedding. She's one of my mother's four sisters."

"I'm afraid I only sorted them out by dress color. Puce, olive, coral and chartreuse."

"She was the plump one."

"Chartreuse."

"I guess." He couldn't be expected to notice what his odd assortment of aunts wore. "Anyway, she's having a family gathering to welcome Tina—and, of course, Dan—back from their honeymoon."

"Short honeymoon."

"They flew to Vegas for a few days. They only took a week off from work."

"Well, Vegas is romantic, I guess." She didn't sound certain. "But I don't think I should intrude on a family dinner."

A minute ago he hadn't wanted to ask her; now he didn't want her to wiggle out of it. Every soldier needed combat training. What if she hooked up with some guy who had a family as rambunctious as his?

"I have a couple of dates, thanks to you for taking me to the reception. But I do have some experience. I've been dating since I got the braces off my teeth."

"I dated a girl with—" No, she didn't need to hear about his adolescent exploits. "Never mind. Can you handle a spaghetti dinner with my clan?"

"I can handle it, but—"

"Good, let's get it over with."

"I didn't say I'd go."

"You didn't say you wouldn't." He smiled broadly, warmly and seductively, throwing all he had into it.

"If that's a triumphant grin—"

"No, just optimistic."

"I don't know, Tom. An extra person for dinner…"

"Not a valid argument. My aunt always cooks enough for an army."

"I'd have to go home and change—"

"No, you wouldn't." All he could see under the pink smock were trim navy pant legs, but betting on her taste in clothes was no gamble. "It's come-as-you-are."

"Where does she live?"

"About half an hour west. Are you ready to go?"

"Won't it be way out of your way to bring me home afterward?"

She wasn't the first female who didn't appreciate freezing her cute little butt off in the VW. "I have the van, and I'm not taking no for an answer."

He'd stripped his gears. He wasn't even sure he

wanted her to go, but here he was maneuvering her into it.

"On one condition."

She did know how to be bad. The lessons must be really paying off.

"I'll follow you there in my car."

"That's not necessary."

"Hey, it's not a date, is it?" She laughed; she had him there.

"No, no, of course not."

"You're sure you don't want to take someone else?"

Did she think he went out every night? Yeah, she probably did, but he was ticked.

"If I did, I wouldn't have asked you."

"Well, okay. I can leave now, but I don't like putting a crimp in your love life."

"Don't worry, I won't let you."

What a lie. He was living like a monk just to help her find a forever-and-ever sucker, and she was passing judgment on his sex life.

He left the store and waited in the van until she came out in her ski jacket and a goofy little hat pulled down over one eyebrow.

Fortunately, his relatives loved unexpected guests. It saved them from having to talk to each other all evening, although his mother and her sisters could wring a couple of hours' conversation out of a case of shingles. Every disease known to mankind had hit someone they knew, and they remembered symptoms better than doctors going up for their licenses.

What was he getting into, taking Julie to a family gathering again so soon? He slapped his forehead and watched her walk to her car, stepping agilely around patches of ice. She had a deliciously cute wiggle, one that invited little squeezes.

Damn, he had to come up with someone better than Peter Carlyle. Talk about putting caviar in the cat's dish! She'd almost be better off with his newly divorced cousin, Ray.

He groaned aloud at the prospect of Ray doing his ear-wiggling trick at dinner while he sucked in long saucy strands of pasta.

As they pulled into traffic, Tom wondered again if taking Julie to see his family was a big mistake.

His aunt Betty and her husband Horace—since his fiftieth birthday, he preferred to be called Bud, but no one in the family remembered—had bought a square box of a house early in their marriage and spent over thirty years embellishing it. Aluminum awnings hung in odd spots, and flower boxes with dead stalks had hearts cut into them. The walk was a maze of leafless hedges, cement garden ornaments and big flower tubs now heaped with snow. He guided Julie to the front door with his hand on her waist, his whole arm vibrating because her walk felt as good as it looked.

The door flew open before they could ring—his aunt's radar in action. He must have been out of his mind bringing her here. His mom and her sisters swooped down on Julie the instant they stepped inside, welcoming her as if she were the homecoming honeymooner—or the girl destined to drag a happy bachelor to his Waterloo.

"Julie, sure I remember you," Aunt Betty gushed. "Come see if you know everybody. We're tickled pink to see you again."

Tom reluctantly trailed behind her; he couldn't desert her while she ran the family gauntlet.

"Of course, I remember you," she was saying to his aunt Pru. "You were wearing that lovely coral dress at the wedding."

His aunt beamed. They liked Julie. He groaned inwardly, wondering what it was about her that brought out his protective urge. And, boy, did he wish that was the only urge she inspired.

Forbidden fruit, he thought unhappily. Just because he'd decided she was off-limits didn't mean he couldn't stop thinking about her in a way that had nothing to do with being a good buddy or a tutor. He caught a glimpse of her perfect breasts under a soft pink sweater and had to wipe his sweaty palms on the sides of his jeans.

She wasn't the most beautiful woman he knew, and he'd dated sexier ones. Maybe it was just the fact that he'd never had a chance to stare into those mesmerizing blue eyes while she was naked. Maybe if he saw all there was to see and felt those luscious curves writhing under him, he wouldn't feel so threatened.

If he didn't watch out, he'd be the one standing at the end of a long aisle in a rented tux watching his life pass before his eyes.

No way! She was gorgeous, but not what he wanted. She wasn't looking for a few nights of fun, and he wasn't going to do the routine with the white picket fence and two-point-four kids. They both knew where they stood, so all he had to do was guide her from first date to altar. A piece of cake. He hoped.

"Put your tongue back in your mouth, dummy!" Tina came up behind him, swatted his arm with one hand, and gestured with a big chunk of Italian bread in the other. ''It's not like you to let it all hang out.''

''What are you talking about?''

''The happy day when you have to eat your words. You know, the garbage about staying wild and free.''

''Haven't you put on a few pounds?'' he teased good-naturedly, attempting to change the subject. ''Shouldn't you be holed up somewhere making a baby instead of chowing down with the relatives?''

''She's the girl who sold you the wedding gown, right? How come she spent most of the night dancing with Peter Carlyle if you're interested? I can't believe he's any serious competition.''

''I can't believe you were checking up on me at your own reception,'' he countered. ''How is married life?''

''Answering a question with a question?'' his twin accused him. ''I know your slippery ways.''

He looked around, realizing she'd backed him into the little alcove Horace had built to display his first—and only—bowling trophy. Now it was a bower of shelves filled with glass baskets and his aunt's collection of Princess Di memorabilia, all lit by dazzling overhead lights.

''I'm only helping her out by giving her some dating advice. She's had bad luck with men, and she's going out with Peter this weekend.''

''Guess I read you wrong.'' It was as close as Tina would come to an apology.

''Your extra pounds only show below the waist,'' he said to even the score.

He had a startling thought. Would Tina turn into one of his aunts?

''I'd better go rescue Julie. Ray is doing his ear-wiggling trick,'' he said, nearly sprinting across the living room to save her.

''Aunt Betty is a terrific cook,'' he said to Julie at the dinner table, trying to suggest a bright side to the ordeal of this family dinner. ''Her menus are a little strange, but everything tastes good.''

Tom ladled some pickled beets and a big purple egg onto his plate beside the spaghetti and wondered why his mother insisted his father come. He rarely came to a gathering of his in-laws.

''Oh, I dropped my napkin,'' Julie whispered.

''I'll get it,'' he said, but it was easier to offer than to do it.

His aunt had put extra leaves in her dining room table, and enough wooden folding chairs for a small funeral were crowded around it. With the wall behind him, he could only wiggle back a couple of inches, so he had to dive and grab.

What he grabbed was slender, firm and shapely.

''Hey, that's my ankle,'' Julie said.

''Sorry.'' He felt his way down her nylon-encased foot, over the toe of her glove-soft shoe, and wiggled his fingers hoping to grab the linen napkin Betty used to mark major occasions.

''I can't find it.'' He came up, his face hot and his palms damp. ''You can have mine.''

''We can share. They're as big as bedsheets.''

''No one who isn't a relative should have to go through this,'' he whispered close to her ear, although it was unlikely anyone could hear him. It took a top-of-the-lungs shout to be heard across the table in the din of several dozen people talking at once. ''Would you like to leave?''

"No, I'm having fun," she said loudly.

Even as she said it, Julie realized it was true. Her family was smaller and widely scattered. Tom's relatives talked too loud, laughed a lot and seemed genuinely fond of each other. They also made her, a stranger, feel welcome and liked, but, of course, she knew what they were hoping: that she was the one who'd put a brand on the family maverick. But she didn't even want to think about that. Tom had made it absolutely clear that commitment and marriage weren't in his plans. And she was still too emotionally fragile to indulge in hopeless infatuations.

In other words, a crush on Tom would be crazy.

Unfortunately her ankle was still tingling, and she didn't mind at all that his leg was caressing hers— but only because they were packed so tightly around the table.

"A toast," Uncle Horace proposed, lifting a precariously full goblet of dark red wine. "To the newlyweds. The honeymoon is over, Danny-boy. She'll be bringing out the leash anytime now."

"Amen to that," Tom said so softly only Julie could hear him.

Horace was as verbose as he was rotund. He kept the toasts going by jumping in whenever there was a lull. Julie made one serving of wine last through the twenty or so rounds of glass-clinking, but the bright lights from the chandelier and the close-packed bodies were making a steam room of the dining area.

When the meal was over, a few people drifted away from the table, and Tom was quick to join them. Julie followed, squeezing behind the chairs blocking them. She had the absolutely shocking thought that Tom couldn't have made it if he'd had an—if he were aroused.

How could she think about him that way? When he put his hand on her upper arm, she jerked it away. They were surrounded by a hoard of his relatives, including his mother, and she was literally vibrating with—

Desire. *Call it what it is,* she chided herself.

Somehow they ended up in the kitchen—alone. Julie was momentarily distracted by the profusion of appliances. The counter was crowded with more small electrical kitchen aids than she'd ever seen outside a store.

Tom read her mind. "Uncle Horace is big on mechanical gadgets. If Betty got anything else for Christmas or her birthday, she'd faint."

Julie stared at the collection of dicers, slicers, cookers, toasters, beaters, heaters and others with mysterious purposes.

"Why three microwaves?"

"In case two malfunction." He grinned, and she giggled. "Let's see if we can find a quiet corner."

"To talk." She was telling herself, not him.

He led the way down red-tiled steps to the basement, but here, too, every inch seemed to be living space. The rec room had a bar and Ping-Pong table, both already in use. Tom led her through a second boxy room, a sewing niche, and opened a closed door, only to find two carrot-headed cousins playing an antique nickel slot machine in another paneled, carpeted room.

"You guys aren't supposed to be playing with that," he said, "but if you're quick about it, you can use the VCR in Uncle Horace's bedroom. Look in the case next to it. I think you'll find a copy of *Space Babes from Planet Q* next to Aunt Betty's five copies of *Saturday Night Fever*.''

''You do have a way with kids,'' she said, laughing when they ran off and banged the door shut behind them. ''Why five copies?''

''My aunt's a Travolta freak.''

''You have an entertaining family.''

''Please...''

''No, I mean it.'' She sat on a threadbare couch, pretending to study the old tin signs hung on knotty-pine walls.

''Well, hopefully we won't have to do this coaching too much longer.''

''No.''

He'd just given her a verbal punch, and she hugged her solar plexus, wondering why it hurt so much.

''What I meant—''

''I know what you meant.''

''No, you don't. I enjoy helping you, but there's only so much I can teach you.'' He shook his head dolefully. ''Sometimes I come across as a dope.''

''A nice dope, though.''

If she ever did find the right man, it would be nice if he looked something like Tom. Mr. Right didn't have to have unruly dark blond hair that invited finger-combing or brown eyes that turned her knees to water, but she did love Brunswick's legs. She could see the swell of muscle in his calf when he rested one ankle on his other knee, and his thighs looked strong and firm in jeans that fit, no doubt by design, like a second skin.

She didn't dare check out below the belt. It was hard enough remembering the way the back seam of his tight denims slipped slightly inward to frame round, hard-packed buns. And his chest—if he ever took his shirt off, she'd probably swoon.

"Your sister looks so happy."

"Yeah."

"Her husband dotes on her."

"Fawns." He made it sound like a sissy thing.

"I don't think I'll ever find someone who's right for me." It was her worst fear, and it just sort of slipped out.

"Hey, don't give up. You've got the world's best coach. And you won't end up with a lapdog like Dan."

"Don't you like your brother-in-law?"

"Sure, I like him. He's one of my best friends."

"Well, I'd hate to hear what you have to say about anyone you don't like!"

"It's not about liking. Dan scampers around like a monkey on a chain. When Tina says jump, he tumbles all over the place. He used to be fun. Now he's a domesticated wimp."

"Maybe he only wants to make Tina happy."

"Yeah, sure." He sounded morose.

"Or maybe you're scared the same thing could happen to you."

"I'm supposed to be doing the counseling." There was no warmth in his grin. "I like my life the way it is."

"Congratulations. Why make only one woman happy when you can spread joy far and wide?"

"Look, Julie, we're really getting off base here. All I'm trying to do is make sure you don't make the same mistakes you did with Brad."

"Ouch!"

"I didn't mean the breakup was your fault."

"But picking a loser was."

"Let's focus on your date—dates—this weekend."

"Sure, why not?" She stared at his hand resting on his knee, wishing it was on her knee, then hated herself for being attracted to another Mr. Wrong.

"On your date," he said with determination, "make sure you end it first. A bad girl always calls the shots. It's over when *you* say it's over. And don't make the first one last too long. Let him think your time is valuable."

"And I'm bestowing a gift on him by sharing a few hours."

"Exactly."

"What if I'm having fun?"

"Be strong. Call the shots. Now about the good-night kiss…"

"I don't want any advice about that."

"I know." His grin was wicked. "All the more reason to follow my rule. Be stingy."

"I thought bad girls liked sex."

"We're not into sex yet—only the first good-night kiss on the cheek."

"Or the forehead?"

He had the grace to look uncomfortable.

"If he goes for your lips, only let him graze them."

"I thought cows grazed. People kiss."

"I hope you're taking this seriously. The worst thing you can do is invite him into your apartment on the first date."

"Tom, your rules sound so old-fashioned. I thought you were going to give me helpful advice."

"If you want plain language, here it is. Most guys are mainly interested in scoring."

"The voice of experience?"

He ignored her comment, his most irritating trait.

"It's the one constant in the male-female thing."

"Relationship, not 'thing.'"

"What men want most is the unattainable—or what they *think* is out of reach."

"I knew that in kindergarten."

She was cross with him but furious at herself. Why on earth was she letting a confirmed bachelor give her advice on how to keep a man? She wasn't even sure she wanted one anymore!

"Knowing and doing aren't the same thing," he said.

"I'm going home."

"You can run away, but you're making a big mistake if you think—"

The overhead neons flickered once, then again.

"Horace needs to rewire this place," Tom complained. "I'll bet those kids are playing with his—"

This time the lights flickered and went out. The windowless cubicle went absolutely black.

They heard a few muted sounds, but the door shut them off from the people in the rec room.

"Where's the switch box?" she asked, instinctively standing even though it didn't seem wise to stumble around in an unfamiliar, dark basement.

"Probably in the furnace area. Someone will take care of it."

She hadn't realized how close he was.

"A bad girl would know what to do now," he said in a husky voice she hadn't heard before.

"Look for a flashlight?"

"Wrong answer."

She reached out and let her hand rest on his chest, hearing and feeling his sharp intake of breath.

"Assuming I'm with someone who's not a potential husband..." she said.

"Then the rules change—a lot."

"A bad girl would take advantage of a blackout."

"I certainly would," he whispered.

She could feel his breath on her forehead, then his lips.

"Are you just warming up?" she challenged brazenly. She moistened her dry lips with the tip of her tongue, then leaned toward him just as his arms circled her, his fingers caressing her back, inching up her sweater.

"Oh..."

His mouth covered hers, making the flesh around it tingle. She parted her lips, ignoring all the reasons why this shouldn't be happening. Her conscience warned her, but she didn't want to stop the sensuous probing of his tongue or the hungry eagerness of his kisses.

He was teasing the snaps on her bra, sliding his finger under the elastic, prolonging the moment when he'd release her breasts from lacy confinement. All his preconceived theories about Julie were dying like burnt-out sparklers. There was nothing he could teach her about fitting her body to his, rubbing against him in a dozen different places, all of them insanely erotic. He felt like a superhero breaking free of a hundred ropes binding his body.

She was the aggressor now, nipping at his lips between breathless little kisses, running her hands over the front of his shirt until she found and teased his nipples.

"Oh..." His moan welled up, and he couldn't wait another moment to hold her breasts in his hands.

"We shouldn't..." she murmured, unresisting when he slid his knee between her legs.

"No, not here..." But he didn't know if he could wait until they drove all the way back to her place.

"Tom..."

The lights came on, harsh neons draining the color from her cheeks but showing him the swollen pink of her lips.

"We can't..." She pulled away, surprising him with the strength behind her panicky retreat.

"We can go to your place."

"No!"

She turned and ran, leaving the door open behind her, sprinting away with the speed of a frightened rabbit.

So much for being a bad girl! he thought with a mixture of amusement and regret, in no state to rush after her through a bunch of curious relatives.

How would she handle her dates if a few kisses from him spooked her enough to turn tail? Of course, he was the one who should be running as far away from Julie Myers as he could get. He hadn't gotten so hot so fast in ages—if ever.

He had his work cut out. He had to make her irresistible to his friends—especially to the marriage-minded ones, scarce as they were—and totally *resistible* to him.

Breathing deeply, he tried to think sobering thoughts and forget the impact she'd had on him.

He found a few nickels in his pocket and stood in front of the old-fashioned gambling machine, glumly feeding his change into the slot and watching cherries, plums and lemons spin to a stop. The one-armed bandit quickly cleaned him out, but he'd had a chance to think.

Yep, he had his work cut out for him. He and some buddies were going to give Julie a surprise or two on girls' night out.

6

——◆——

"What's this sudden urge to bowl?" Buck Kelly asked from the back seat in Tom's van. "I thought we were going to shoot some pool at Ernie's."

"We can do that later," Tom said.

Buck wasn't easily put off. "I thought you didn't like bowling."

"I just want to check someone out, then we can leave," Tom said, trying to explain as little as possible. "I didn't expect you to come with us tonight, Dan."

"Tina took a flight to London for a friend who's sick. Her week's vacation is up, anyway," he said morosely.

"Hey, cheer up, good buddy." Buck reached over the seat and squeezed Dan's shoulder. "A married man needs a little time off, but I'm surprised Tina let you call me."

"She doesn't tell me what I can do. All she said was, 'Stay away from my troublemaking brother.'"

"Sweet kid," Tom said. "I tried to warn you."

"You can't tell a man in luvvvv anything," Buck joked. "Hey, I bet the astronauts can see that sign from the shuttle."

Lights from the huge Bowl-O-Rama sign made the

interior of the van as light as day when Tom drove past it to the crowded parking area.

"Looks like the place to be," Buck said.

"Don't embarrass me, guys," Dan pleaded. "No honeymoon jokes, no trying to fix me up with some bimbo."

"We're too mature for that," Buck assured him with mock gravity.

Tom led the way inside, and saw just what he'd expected: a whole lot of babes pretending they were there to bowl, and just as many guys not bothering to pretend. It was a cattle call and a good place to see if Julie was going to put any bad-girl practices into effect, if she was there. Who could predict what one woman would do, let alone a gang of them?

He was still edgy from the lights-out incident the night before, but he wasn't sure Julie belonged in a bar crowd like this. She was sweet and naive, but so damn sexy some jerk was sure to take advantage of her someday. Her sexiness came from not knowing how desirable she was. If she could learn to play that up, she'd have men dropping at her feet like flies. But was she ready for it?

Was he?

"Check that out!" Buck whistled softly, and nudged Tom. "Is she stacked or what?"

"Hey, grow up," Dan said.

Tom agreed, but he'd called Buck because the guy would go anywhere and try anything. Of all his friends, Buck had resisted growing up the hardest.

"I'll put our names down for a lane," Dan offered.

"You two go ahead. I'll just look around," Tom said, leaving his friends by the counter.

He hadn't been here before, but the layout was typical: a raised level behind the lanes with booths where people could eat, drink and watch the bowlers, and rows of seats on the lower level by the electronic scorekeepers.

He could feel his pulse beating in his throat and blamed it on the noisy impact of balls on pins. Instead of following the usual procedures, the management assigned alleys on a first-come basis, mixing people up, which was the whole idea of a singles' night. Julie's group could be split up, sharing alleys with some predatory males.

He checked out lane after lane, beginning to think he was wasting his time. Then he saw her.

Buck and Dan caught up with him, and he led the way down to the area behind the bowlers.

"We'll probably have a half hour wait," Dan said.

Tom scarcely heard what his friends were saying; he was too busy thinking of what he'd say to Julie. She might not be pleased to see him—especially after last night.

He sat down behind her group, in no hurry to be noticed. She was with a tall, slender girl who wore her hair in a severe bun with a huge silver bow and, surprise, surprise, a pair of strawberry-blond twins with freckles and thick single braids down their backs. Both were wearing tight black jeans and horizontally striped tops, differing only in that one top was blue and yellow, the other green and yellow. They were cute girls, but he couldn't take his eyes off Julie.

She was wearing a short split skirt—didn't she know it was freezing cold outside?—and her legs were spectacular, even in clunky red and blue bowling shoes and white anklets.

Dan left for the concession stand, and Buck wan-dered off to check out a blonde a few alleys away. Tom only wanted to see how Julie handled herself in a sizzling singles scenario.

She seemed intent on her game, which was more than he could say for the guys using the next lane. They were doing everything but handstands to attract the women's attention. Their antics made Tom feel tired and jaded—and too old for their game.

Dan came back with a huge cardboard tray of chili fries, sat down and started wolfing them. Would marriage change his buddy into an Uncle Horace with fat rolls and kooky hobbies? Dan wouldn't be his first married friend to get on the fast track to middle-age. He was glad his sister had a nice husband, but he was more determined than ever not to become a domesticated couch potato himself.

Tom didn't know what irritated him more: the guys hitting on Julie and her friends, or Julie not taking advantage of the situation to practice flirting. She didn't have to be a bad girl—and she probably never would be one—to exercise her feminine wiles. From what he could see, she was being friendly but not at all encouraging with the guys. If she really wanted their attention, she should ask for their help instead of trying to out-bowl them. She could take lessons from the twin in green stripes.

When it was Julie's turn again, he got up and sauntered over, speaking first to the twin in green.

"Hi, I'm a twin myself. Do you two ever go to the twin conventions?" he asked.

Not that he'd ever gone to one himself! Tina would rather join a polar bear club and do the January dive into Lake Michigan than show up at a two-by-two event with him.

Julie was picking up her ball, but she turned suddenly when she heard his voice, bouncing it back on the rack where it narrowly missed falling off onto her foot. She nodded stiffly and stepped up to the line for her turn, rolling an almost-perfect gutter ball.

"We go to a convention almost every year," the more gregarious twin enthused. "I practically have to drag Tanya, but we both have a blast."

Julie was embarrassed by her bad roll and furious at Tom for hitting on her friends. All three were clustered around him, chattering like mindless bimbos. She finished her turn, the second ball a split that left two pins standing.

"Julie, meet Tom. He's a twin," Monica said, making no move to take her turn.

"Yes, I know him—and his twin sister," she said, glad to burst their bubble with the knowledge that there weren't two like him.

"Where have you been hiding this gorgeous man?" This from Karen, her oldest and dearest friend. "You're up, Monica."

They finished the game, their second and the worst Julie had bowled in years. The ball wasn't the only thing she was struggling to control under Tom's watchful eye. She was so angry her blood seemed to be boiling.

What the devil was he doing, trailing her on girls' night out? Did it have anything to do with the disastrous dinner last night?

Tanya started the third game, but Julie bowed out.

"I've had enough," she said, "but you three go ahead."

"Let me buy you a drink," Tom offered, taking her elbow none too gently and steering her toward the concession stand where she saw Dan buying a plate of nachos and cheese.

"What's he doing here?" she asked, recognizing the newlywed with surprise. "And what about you? I never should've told you we were coming here. I can't believe you were hitting on my friends!"

He answered the easy question first. "Tina took a flight to London for a sick friend."

"And the two of you just happened to stop here?"

"No, we're with another friend. I think he's bowling. I was only introducing myself to your friends. I came to observe you."

"Observe me!"

He ordered sodas for both of them and handed her a tall cup. Her first impulse was to dump it where it would do him some good, but her mother had taught her to be a lady in public.

"It seemed like a good idea. Think about it." He drank some soda, probably to give him time to concoct a story. "Isn't girls' night out just an opportunity for you and your friends to meet guys?"

"Not necessarily. Don't you and your friends do anything but try to meet women?"

"Right now, you're the one they most want to meet. You made quite an impression at the wedding. But if you don't make a permanent connection through me, you'll be back on your own again. Face it, you're not very adept at meeting eligible men."

"Thank you for boosting my confidence," she said in a tone icier than the contents of her cup.

She sipped at the soda so she wouldn't have to meet his eyes. How could she be having this conversation after last night? It was bad enough he'd kissed her; she was mortified that she'd kissed him—touched him—and had wanted him to continue kissing her.

Everything had changed between them. She couldn't go on pretending he was only an acquaintance trying to help her out.

"I'm only trying to help you," he said, as if reading her mind.

He said it with such sincerity, she wanted to believe him. She did believe him in a way.

"About last night…" She led the way to a spot at the back where no one could overhear.

"I'm really sorry."

"You're sorry?"

"Being buddies with a woman is tough." He grinned sheepishly. "Especially one as cute as you."

She felt a warm glow; maybe their friendship wasn't completely ruined.

"The wine—"

"Had nothing to do with it," he said with a mischievous grin. "You nursed one glass through all of Uncle Horace's toasts. That's probably a family record."

"You noticed?"

"Yeah, I noticed."

She could feel his eyes on her, but she still couldn't look directly into his face. What if he thought she was interested in him? Was he encouraging her to meet more men to emphasize that he wasn't available?

"About your techniques…"

She drank more soda, pretty sure she wasn't going to like his analysis, then said, "What techniques?"

"That's what I'm talking about. You don't have any." He glanced around. "Down there, by lane seven. Look at the woman getting lessons from one of the guys who was coming on to your friends.''

''He was obnoxious. I do have some standards.''

She watched a very well-endowed woman in tight black leggings and a rhinestone-studded T-shirt getting lessons. She was tossing back her long platinum hair, making helpless gestures, arching her back, giving him the works.

''I've seen her here before. She's a league bowler with a high average. She can roll the ball hard enough to splinter the pins. Are you telling me I should pretend to be helpless?''

''No, I'm just pointing out the way a bad girl operates.''

''Sure, it's easy to be a bad girl when you have the right equipment.''

''It's not what you have. It's what you do with it.''

He took her elbow again and guided her back down to the lanes, stopping within sight of the alley where her friends were still bowling.

''One of the twins is a bad girl. The other isn't.''

''That's ridiculous! They're identical twins. You have to know them pretty well to know which is Monica and which is Tanya.''

''Stay here. I'll be right back.''

He went to the concession stand, then returned with three sodas and carried them over to her friends.

She didn't know what he was trying to prove, but she was skeptical about the whole charade.

He handed a cup to each of them as they moved away from the lanes, their last game completed. Karen and Tanya both reached for their purses, smiling their thanks when Tom refused to be reimbursed.

Monica accepted his offering, sucking slowly on

the straw. Even from where she was standing, Julie could see her friend was batting her lashes.

She was flabbergasted. She'd been friends with the twins since junior high. How could she have missed that Monica had probably traded in her practical cotton underwear for silk teddies? Was this her subconscious reason for liking Tanya a little more than her twin?

Tom's two friends joined them, and the seven of them crowded into one of the larger booths. Monica, she noticed, managed to squeeze between Dan and Buck, the friend Julie remembered by sight from the wedding but didn't remember talking to.

Tom disappeared for a few minutes, then came back carrying a tub of popcorn and wearing the alley's red and black shoes. He put popcorn on the table but didn't give her a chance to eat any.

"Now do you see the difference between the twins?" he asked, after taking her hand and pulling her away from the group.

"I'm afraid you're going to explain it to me anyway."

He was.

"They're both cute, but Monica takes what's offered as her due because she's attractive. That, in turn, makes her more attractive."

"Because she takes things as her due?"

"You've got it."

"I don't see how this has anything to do with me. Is there going to be a quiz later?"

"Come on, time for some more lessons."

"On attracting men?" She'd about had it on that subject.

"Nope, bowling lessons. There's a lull. We can use lane nineteen."

"I didn't think you were here for the sport."

He put his arm around her shoulders, forgetting how much he disliked rented shoes.

"You first." He gestured, sitting back to watch her.

"You've already seen me bowl a gutter ball."

She looked flushed and uncomfortable, but he smiled encouragement, pleased when she made a spare.

"Pretty good," he said. "But let me give you some pointers."

He stood behind her and helped her position the ball, keeping one hand on her waist, his fingers splayed over her hipbone. Her hair was so close he could detect the subtle floral scent of her shampoo and see where a few moist strands clung to her neck under her ponytail.

"Hold yourself like this." He slid his hand over one shoulder, caressing her upper arm below the short sleeve of her bright peach knit top.

"I don't think this stance is going to help my game," she said in a husky whisper that sent ripples down his spine.

"Trust me."

"This reminds me of dancing at the wedding."

"Now when you release the ball…" he continued, keeping up the pretense of teaching because it felt so pleasant to have his arm around her.

"Are you trying to attract other men for me? Is this the bowling alley version of dirty dancing?" she asked less softly, pulling away.

"I'm teaching you how to take lessons. Men love being instructors."

"Well, Mr. Teacher, you're up. Let's see if you can throw this thing yourself."

He went to the rack, grabbed a heavier ball, and threw it with more force than finesse.

He got lucky: a strike.

"Show-off," she groused. "I'll bet you can't do that again."

In the next frame she rattled him into missing a split. She got another spare. Her bowling wasn't sensational, but it was good—very good by his standards. He wasn't at all sure he could beat her.

She goaded him into making it a real contest. The shoes hurt his feet, and the ball didn't feel right, but he couldn't give her the satisfaction of hearing him make excuses. He had to struggle to come out ahead one-eighty-seven to one-seventy-six at the end of the game.

"Were you trying to make a point?" she asked as he willingly conceded one game was enough.

"You've made it for me. If you want to attract men, it helps to feign a little helplessness."

"The kind of act that worked for girls in high school?"

"Something like that."

"Then fall into bed with the captain of the football team?"

"No! Definitely not! If you're easy, there's no challenge."

"But I should be the kind of girl who blows the last frame so the guy can win?"

"You didn't?" He had a sneaking suspicion she had.

"You'll never know, will you?"

Actually, she was beginning to understand exactly

what he meant, but his lessons were depressing her. She doubted she could ever be anything but herself— a nice, dull, average person.

They walked to the counter, and she refused to let him pay for her games.

"Your bad-girl quotient just dropped from C-minus to D-plus," he teased. "Next we'll work on being mysterious and alluring."

"Just what I need."

What she really needed was an aspirin, but she was the one who'd asked for his help in the first place. What would really be helpful was if Tom suddenly turned into a frog so she could concentrate more on the lessons and less on the devastatingly sexy teacher.

"Let me help you with your shoes," he said, leading her to a bench and getting down on one knee to unlace the clunky bowling shoes.

He took his time, lifting her foot to slide off the right shoe but hanging on to her ankle for longer than necessary.

"You're wearing hose under your socks," he said, running the tips of his fingers over her calf.

"Cold out," she managed to explain between gulps of air, dropping her boots out of their bag.

He bent over the left shoe, and was even slower in removing it, his tousled hair so close she had to squeeze her fingers into fists to keep from checking its softness. Tom was the kind of man who made a girl forget she'd vowed to wait until marriage to make love. All she could think about was being naked with this man someplace other than a bowling alley—or his aunt's basement. Their kisses last night seemed chaste compared to the images dancing through her head.

He sat so close to her to remove his own shoes, she was afraid he was thinking the same thing she was. But that couldn't be; she was a project, not a woman, in his eyes. If he could read her thoughts... She blushed in spite of the impossibility.

"I think my friends are ready to leave," she said. Her voice sounded different in her own ears. He must have heard the strange sultry quality, too. He put his arm around her shoulders and pressed against her side, his thigh as firm and strong as she remembered.

"They'll wait."

"I should get my coat."

"I'll get it for you."

She handed over her claim tag and waited while he retrieved her navy coat. He was already wearing his bomber jacket, which was open, reminding her how hard his chest was, how flat his stomach, how lean his waist. She glanced lower, and he caught her. There was a noticeable bulge in his pants.

"That's the sexiest thing I've seen you do," he said softly, stepping behind her to hold her coat.

Thank heavens she couldn't see his face! Hers was probably flaming red.

"My friends are waiting," she reminded him.

"Be bad tonight. Do what you want."

"I want to leave," she lied.

"They'll wait."

"But—"

"Let's give them something to talk about while they're waiting."

He spun her around, giving her a glimpse of the twins' lavender and blue jackets, then his lips came down on hers.

In bowling it would have been a strike that scattered the pins into the next lane. He kissed her full on the mouth, his tongue parting her lips, the force of it vibrating all the way to her toes.

She was breathless, wanting more, and she hadn't even had a chance to kiss him back.

"Good night." His words caressed her ears; she'd never heard a voice so compellingly sensual.

She reached out, weak with longing, and needing something more from him to cushion their separation.

But he was already on his way out.

Tom left as quickly as possible without actually sprinting. Halfway to the exit he spotted his friends and gave them an offhanded wave to follow, but he didn't wait. He needed to cool down fast before he did something with consequences he wasn't ready to face.

He was being an arrogant bastard, trying to teach Julie how to be sexy. She packed a wallop that had nothing to do with tricks or techniques.

Sitting in the van waiting for his friends, he fumed at himself for being so vulnerable to her innocence.

On the way home talking to his friends was about as much fun as small talk with a dentist who was about to start drilling. They were curious; they'd seen, too. He had to take some ribbing, but he'd never been less in the mood for male-bonding.

He dropped his friends off and got back to his apartment before he let himself rerun the whole evening in his mind.

In spite of his good intentions, he hadn't even touched on the first-date stuff. He'd gotten Julie into this thing with Peter, a guy with a rep for going head-over-heels with every girl he dated. Julie didn't need any coaching to attract Peter; she needed a course in self-defense. He'd have his hand under her skirt before she noticed his drooling.

He'd blown it tonight.

Had she really let him win?

He wasn't sure he liked this bad-girl business.

7

"Think about Peter, Peter, Peter," Julie chanted.

She felt like a witch casting a spell, but the only one she was trying to enchant was herself—Julie Myers, single working girl. This wasn't her usual way of psyching herself up for a first date, but she was having a hard time remembering how Peter looked. His image drifted somewhere in the fog-shrouded recesses of her mind, but when she tried to focus on it, he came through with Tom's face.

It was all Brunswick's fault—well, mostly his fault. Okay, partly his fault. A man whose kisses had real oomph—not Jerry-Poomph-oomph—shouldn't scatter them around like unguided missiles.

She pressed a palm against her mouth, in her mind erasing the sweetly sensual sensation of his lips on hers. It was hopeless. The only way she was going to get Tom out of her mind was to have a wonderful time with Peter.

She was determined to have that great time—if she ever made up her mind what to wear. She glanced at the nightstand clock as she sat on the edge of the bed struggling to make panty hose roll smoothly over slightly damp legs.

They were going to dinner. Dinner was nice. She wasn't familiar with the restaurant where Peter had made reservations, but Misty Shores Inn suggested candlelight and romantic music.

She slipped into her best bra, leaning over to fill the cups before snapping it in back. Why was she getting ready so early? Something about a last-minute rush always pumped her up, made her ready for a terrific date—or a terrible one. Now she was probably going to be ready too early, and that meant pacing and waiting, letting doubts grow into panic.

''First dates are the pits,'' she said, peering into the dresser mirror.

Her long, dark hair was still slightly damp, but she brushed it into the smooth style that framed her face in what she liked to call her Botticelli look. She wasn't big on heavy makeup; mascara and a trace of eye shadow, plus lipstick, did it for her. She applied her favorite cherry-red lip gloss, bright and slightly daring, and wondered if Tom would call it a bad-girl color.

Darn! Tom Brunswick didn't write the book on attracting a man. Why did his advice keep popping into her head?

She checked her makeup one more time, dabbed her only expensive perfume on her throat, earlobes, and the hollow between her breasts, then hoped she hadn't overdone it.

Tom would probably suggest wearing the sexy little number she'd bought for the wedding, but she couldn't wear a dress Peter had already seen on their first date. Regardless of what Brunswick thought, she did know the finer points of dressing for successful dates.

In a decisive mood now, she zeroed in on her next-newest dress, an emerald green knit with a conservative turtleneck and long sleeves. On the positive side, it was long and clingy with side slits that showed leg. She laid it on the bed, then studied her labeled shoeboxes on the closet shelf. How tall was Peter?

She tried to remember dancing with him, but when she looked up in her daydream, her partner always had Tom's slightly crooked smile and warm brown eyes.

''Oh, darn!''

She chose her low-heeled black pumps, not that she was tall but her dressy three-inch spikes might make her as tall as Peter.

She'd just slithered into the dress and stepped into her shoes when the buzzer sounded. Either her clock was wrong or Peter was making the most annoying faux pas of all: he was early.

''Hello,'' she said with forced cheerfulness.

''It's me, Tom.''

''What are you doing here?''

''Can I come up?''

She wanted to tell him to get lost—she really did—but her treacherous finger responded automatically to his deep voice, even distorted as it was by the apartment's cheap intercom. He was on his way up before she had enough presence of mind to tell him to get lost.

Maybe he was here to apologize for kissing her. What an insult that would be—not to mention a colossal turnoff. It was just what she needed to stop wishing he were her date instead of Peter.

She adjusted her dress in front of the mirror, checked to be sure no panty line showed and went to the door. In practically no time he knocked, but she counted slowly to twenty before opening the door.

"Your timing isn't so good," she said, feigning mild irritation so he wouldn't know how he really affected her.

"It's the best I could do. Had some last-minute business."

Not the grin. Please, not the grin!

He smiled, and her armor crashed around her, leaving her pathetically vulnerable to his brand of charm.

He'd done it again—sluffed off a question.

"What are you doing here?"

"I wanted to see you before your date. Make sure I covered all the first-date rules."

"Tom, you've done that ad nauseam!"

He didn't mention kissing her. She wondered if he would apologize. No, that would be worse than not mentioning it at all, but it did seem that a passionate kiss in a public place called for some kind of commentary.

"Everything is cool. I'm on top of it," she said. At least she had been until he'd come around with his windblown hair and the shadow of bristle on his strong, masculine chin.

"The important thing…" he said, flopping down on her couch with his legs outstretched in tight, faded jeans, "is not to invite him into your apartment. A come-up on the first date can backfire."

"Tom! I'm a bad girl now, remember? A very bad girl. I make the rules."

"Most of the bad girls I know are single."

"You could have a great career as a matchmaker—or host of a dating game."

"Just trying to help."

He stood and circled around her, deciding he was crazy to let her waste such dynamite good looks on Carlyle.

"I can handle this. Like I said, I've been on lots of first dates."

She unconsciously fluffed her hair. That little gesture alone was enough to drive him nuts.

"Did they all lead to second dates?" He should bite his tongue. He'd come to be helpful, not to shake her confidence.

"I didn't want them to."

He liked the touch of haughtiness in her voice. In fact, he liked too darn many things about her. That dress, for instance. It wasn't flashy, but it hugged her curves and showed a good slice of leg. Peter would salivate, and that prospect really bothered him.

"That's the attitude. Be selective."

Face it, Brunswick, he thought, you may hate the idea of wasting her on a guy like Peter, but she has to get into circulation before she can hook up with a wedding-bells type. It was the only way he'd ever get her out of his mind. He'd been crazy to kiss her last night. How much sleep had he lost thinking about those bright red lips parting under his?

To preserve his sanity—and his much-valued bachelorhood—he had to make sure her first date led to other dates that led to commitment, preferably with someone besides lover-boy Carlyle.

He took off his bomber jacket and tossed it over the back of her rocking chair, a necessary step in his somewhat crazy plan.

She did the hair thing again. Did he make her nervous? He kinda liked the idea that he did, but it wasn't why he was here.

"I forgot my earrings!"

She made it sound like a potential disaster. He watched—oh, did he watch—as she hurried into her bedroom. He wanted to help her look for them; even more, he wanted to be the one to fasten the pair of dangly earrings to her delicate lobes. Neither was a good idea. Her perfume was wafting around him, an airborne aphrodisiac, and he didn't know how it would affect him if he got too close to her.

Maybe he was a dope to give up another date night trying to coach Julie into being bad enough to attract men but smart enough to find a keeper.

What really unnerved him was that no other woman appealed to him right now. It probably was a mistake to sacrifice his own social life to help Julie, but she was on his mind all the time.

Hey, it's been a long dry spell, he thought sullenly. *Maybe what you need, Brunswick, is to—*

No, his experience with Brenda was still too fresh in his mind. He'd turned down an all-night ride to paradise with no strings attached just because Julie was preying on his mind. He had to see her hooked up with someone else to kick his libido back into overdrive.

He felt as if he were sending Little Red Riding Hood out to meet the wolf, and he hadn't even liked fairy tales when he was a kid unless they had fire-breathing dragons.

Julie had had less trouble the first time she put earring wires through her newly pierced fourteen-year-old lobes. When they were finally in, she had to do something a whole lot harder—get rid of Tom before Peter showed up.

As soon as she returned into the living room, she knew it was too late. This time the buzzer had to be her date.

"Want me to answer?" Tom asked in a laid-back drawl that only annoyed her.

"Absolutely not!"

She made sure it was Peter, then gave him directions to her apartment although it would be hard not to find it at the top of the stairs.

"You've got to hide," she said urgently.

"Why?"

"Peter can't find you here!"

"Why not?"

"You can be maddening! Please don't do this!"

For some perverse reason, he was enjoying her predicament. But she was right, and he knew it. Her chance of having a good first date was nil if Peter found him there, but he wanted to see what she'd do to persuade him.

"Hide!" she ordered in a no-nonsense tone.

He resisted snapping to attention to mock her command, but he did amble slowly toward her bedroom. Boy, was she sexy when she was mad!

"Didn't I tell you to meet your date in the vestibule instead of letting him come up here?" he asked, trying not to grin at her from the doorway.

"I planned to, until my overbearing coach showed up and interrupted my getting-ready time."

"Sorry about that, but you couldn't look better."

"Tom, please!" she begged in a throaty whisper even though Peter hadn't had time to sprint the two flights to her door.

"I'll let myself out after you leave," he promised, taking pity on her anxiety. "Have fun." But not too much.

He went into her bedroom and closed the door behind him, hoping he wouldn't be there long. The air was moist and fragrant, an extraordinary blend of steam from the adjoining shower and her perfume. He felt a little light-headed, and it had everything to do with imagining her in lacy lingerie, hurrying to get ready on time.

He could hear too well through the thin door. It was almost more than he could stomach when Peter came in and started gushing over how great she looked.

Peter overdid the compliments, but Julie accepted them graciously. She planned to have a great evening, and that meant forgetting Tom's advice—and Tom himself!

"I made reservations for seven," her date reminded her unnecessarily.

He had a young voice, or maybe it was a little high for a man. It reminded her of the lineup of awkward adolescents who'd showed up at her door during her high school days. She'd never refused the offer of a first date; in retrospect, Tom's advice was probably on target. She should have been more discriminating, but she was too softhearted. It took a lot of courage for some high school guys to ask a girl out the first time, so she'd always felt obligated to say yes.

"I'm all ready," she assured Peter. She went to her entryway closet and realized she had a dilemma. The dress was longer than her coat. Would it look silly hanging out? Should she wear her waist-length ski jacket? It would probably look better, but they were going to a fancy restaurant. She remembered Tom hiding in her bedroom, and grabbed her navy coat, slipping into it before Peter could help her. Let him show off his manners at the restaurant. She wasn't at all sure Tom could be trusted to stay out of sight.

Peter wasn't as tall as she'd remembered, at least six inches shorter than Tom. With low, chunky heels she was eyeball-to-eyeball with him, but that didn't prejudice her against him. Size was no big deal. There was a natural kinkiness in his professionally styled russet-colored hair. She wasn't sure what color his eyes were, but he had cute dimples and wore a sharply pressed suit and a tailored black overcoat.

In the parking lot he took her arm so she wouldn't slip on an icy patch, then opened the door of his new model Buick for her. She did remember that he had a good sense of humor and wore a nice spicy after-shave. This promised to be a great first date if she could stop thinking about the man cooling his heels in her bedroom.

Tom came out of hiding as soon as the door closed behind the happy daters. He went into the kitchen and helped himself to a drink of water, hoping to wash away the sour taste in his mouth. No wonder Carlyle got engaged so often. His flowery compliments put up a smoke screen around his dorky personality.

Hey, go easy on the guy, Tom reprimanded himself. You liked him okay before he started sniffing around Julie.

He slammed the glass down so hard he was lucky it didn't shatter in his hand.

His mood improved a little when he went into the living room for his jacket. Had Peter been so dazzled by Julie he hadn't noticed it? Tom grinned wickedly. He hadn't left it there on purpose, but now that he thought of it, why worry? He couldn't seriously see Julie falling for Pete's brand of baloney.

He reached into his jacket pocket and found his car keys, then dropped them as planned behind the rocker. He was smirking when he let Julie's door lock behind him.

It might be a long wait. He sat on the floor in front of her apartment, thankful for the relatively new carpeting in the hallway, and leaned against her door. After a restless night and a long hard day unloading furniture, he was tired enough to doze off anywhere. He closed his eyes, congratulating himself on his cunning.

* * *

Julie threw herself into her role as a charming companion. She remembered Tom's advice even when she tried to block it: laugh at Peter's jokes, but not too heartily.

Peter made it easy for her to be congenial—opening doors, helping with her coat, pulling out her chair, even ordering for her. She was able to sit back and let him do all the work. All she had to do was be alluring and mysterious.

"Naturally the first thing Willard did when he got to the office was..."

Julie could feel her eyes glazing over. If there was a point to Peter's long, involved story about something that had happened at the real estate office where he worked, she hoped she was alert enough to catch it. The only thing worse than not laughing at a funny story was laughing at the wrong time.

Their waiter—or server, as he called himself—was tall and broad-shouldered. He probably made great tips at the upscale restaurant, but he took his job a little too seriously, hovering over them while they tasted the wine and sampled their shrimp cocktails. He wore his hair in a tail, and she wondered if Tom's was long enough to tie back. Probably not, but their waiter had long legs and a tight, muscular butt that reminded her so strongly of Tom she had to study her place setting whenever he turned his back to the table.

Darn you, Tom Brunswick! she thought with a flash of anger.

It was all his fault she wasn't enjoying a pleasant date with a nice guy who wasn't afraid of being courteous to a woman. She didn't want to be thinking of Tom while Peter worked hard to entertain her.

She tried harder to follow the gist of his stories. Maybe this was what marriage was all about: being a sounding board, a good listener and supporter of your man. Unfortunately, she wanted more from life. She wanted excitement, challenge, romance. Completely against her will, she conjured up an image of Tom stripped to the waist with a dueling sword in hand. He was the stuff of heroes, thrilling and sensual but beyond domestication.

"So we all had a good laugh over that," Peter said, concluding a story.

She smiled broadly, trying to make up for missing the punch line. Well, he couldn't expect her to roar with laughter over the antics of people she didn't know.

She felt obligated to show appreciation for the meal, and her fresh salmon steak poached in cream made it easy. The food was delicious and served with flair.

When Peter went into raptures over the dessert tray, she let him order a slice of raspberry cheesecake for her. Her stomach was probably pouching under her form-hugging dress, but her date had a little overhang of his own, not that it was all that noticeable or objectionable, but the "Tom thing" was still plaguing her. *His* midsection was lean and sexy.

She perked up over dessert when Peter steered the conversation to his past fiancées.

"I guess you're curious about my four engagements," he said a little sheepishly.

She encouraged him by describing the way Brad had practically left her at the altar. Tom wouldn't like it, but she had to be herself even if it meant ignoring his taboos.

On the other hand, Peter looked mildly shocked. Apparently she'd tarnished her luster by admitting she'd once been dumped, never mind that her date had been dumped three times and backed off himself once.

"Some people aren't lucky at love," he said, sipping his decaf. "And, of course, some people just aren't ready to commit."

He made a point of telling her he was. Apparently he'd decided to forgive her one dumping. How big of him!

They lingered. She smiled and tried to be entertaining and witty. Maybe she succeeded. Peter seemed to be having a good time.

She was the one who'd been a real jerk on this date. Peter was a sweet, nice-looking guy with a good job, and he wasn't altar-shy. She was the lousy date, eating his scrumptious meal while she let Tom intrude on her thoughts. She had to stop thinking about a man who broke out in hives at the mere mention of the "M" word.

She wanted to meet a nice man and settle down; it was natural for a good relationship to progress to marriage if two people loved each other. Could she settle for less? Would she settle for Tom on any terms he wanted?

The waiters wanted their table, and she couldn't even pretend to sip more decaf.

"I really should go home now," she suggested with what she hoped was a sweet smile of regret.

"I've kept you here forever talking your ear off," he said apologetically.

"No, I've had a wonderful time." At least the stories about his ex-fiancées were riveting stuff—good soap opera material.

"It doesn't have to end. I know a club where we could dance—no hard rock or deafening noise."

She politely demurred.

He didn't push it.

She didn't mind taking Tom's advice about calling the evening to a close while it was still early. The heavy meal and uninterrupted flow of conversation had made her sleepy.

Had she made a connection with Peter? She wasn't sure, but she didn't hate him. What did she expect? That they'd be falling head-over-heels in love after one date?

On the drive home, she was grateful for his endless store of small talk. He'd really demanded very little of her on this date, only that she be a good listener. If she fell short on this, at least she'd covered well with smiles and appropriate questions.

"Can I walk you up?" he asked at the outside entrance to her apartment.

"No, thank you, but I've had a lovely time, Peter."

"It's no trouble—I need the exercise after that dinner."

"Thanks anyway, but not tonight."

He didn't insist; score one for him. Leaning forward, he planted a good-night peck somewhere in the vicinity of her chin, then left with a hearty, "I'll call you."

Her ordeal was over. What should have been a pleasant evening wasn't, and it was all Tom's fault. Why did he have to show up and remind her of what a sexy, appealing man he was? Darn, she had a crush on the man! No matter how much she tried denying it to herself, she'd taken his bait even though it wasn't intended for her.

Nothing could come of it, but it put a damper on every other relationship she might attempt to develop. Somehow she had to be realistic and put him out of her mind. Tom Brunswick was definitely not a one-woman man, and she wasn't interested in being flavor of the month, week or hour.

She climbed the stairs, feeling as though lead weights were strapped to her ankles. Where did she go from here with Peter or any other man? Somehow she had to get Tom out of her system, but how could she when he was always dropping in on her?

She fished for her keys on the way up and was so focused on her problem that she nearly fell over the long legs stretched across the hallway.

"What on earth!"

Tom jerked his head up, then got to his feet, yawning and stretching.

"Your floor gets hard."

She hoped rubbing his butt made him feel better because it certainly made her uncomfortable.

"What are you doing here?" She was fighting mad this time.

"I couldn't leave."

He saw her expression and quickly explained. "I'm not here to check on you," he lied, pulling out the lining of his jacket pockets as proof. "The van keys must have fallen out when I threw my jacket on your chair. I didn't notice until the door locked after me. Guess I fell asleep waiting."

"Oh, great."

Did she buy his story? If she did, she wasn't happy about it.

"What if I'd invited Peter up?"

"You didn't." He couldn't quite conceal his grin of relief.

"No, I followed your advice. I was mysterious, alluring, and hard-to-get."

"Did you have a good time?"

"Marvelous!" She said it in a tone usually reserved for stomping on a spider.

"Well, can I come in and look for my keys?"

"They'd better be there," she warned.

His mother used to have the same expression before she took out her wooden spoon and threatened to whop his butt.

Julie led the way, slipping off her shoes and coat in one fluid movement, abandoning the former where they lay and throwing her coat over the desk chair.

He expected her to help look; in fact, he was looking forward to it. He'd placed the keys behind the rocker, as concealed as they could be if they'd fallen accidentally. He wouldn't mind seeing her bend, and maybe even get down on her hands and knees to look, a little reward for his uncomfortable nap.

Instead she curled up on the couch, pulling up her legs and hugging her knees.

The keys could wait; he wanted to cuddle beside her, nuzzle her neck, find out for himself if her thighs were as firm as they looked.

Her expression wasn't inviting, but he didn't want to leave until he knew how the date had gone. As her tutor, he should be curious, but he didn't want her to know he cared as much as he did.

"How'd it go?" he asked casually.

"Fine."

By telling him so little, she made him even more eager to know if Peter had made any moves on her. But no way would he let her know how personal his interest was.

"We had a very pleasant evening," she added.

Pleasant! Weather was pleasant. She wasn't telling him anything about the date.

"And?"

She told him what they'd had to eat, as if he cared about the menu! She mentioned that Peter was charming and witty—he didn't like that at all.

"And that just about sums up the evening," she said after telling him practically nothing.

She was resting her chin on her knees, keeping them locked together for modesty but not doing anything to quench his imagination. Did she wear panties in rainbow colors or pure white? He could have checked her drawers after she'd left, but he was no snoop. Anyway, there was no substitute for hands-on information.

His exasperation finally got the better of him. "Did he kiss you?"

"A little peck."

"On the lips?"

"Close."

"What does that mean, 'close'?"

She uncoiled, but not without revealing a long expanse of leg that gave him another unwanted jolt.

"Sort of like this." She stood on tiptoes, put her hands on his shoulders to stretch even taller, and planted a light kiss on his chin.

"Just in case you were wondering," she purred without moving away.

Her breasts were lightly brushing his chest, the contact like two electric charges. She was teasing, and he probably had it coming. Maybe she didn't buy his story about the keys, or maybe she was practicing her bad-girl persona on him.

He kept his arms stiff at his sides, not leaning toward her even though it took every ounce of self-control he possessed.

"Yeah, I was wondering."

He wanted to shake her composure, re-establish the coach-player relationship, but his tongue felt thick and he didn't know what to do with his hands.

"Wondering whether I followed your advice?"

Her perfume was heady stuff. He urgently wanted to discover the secret places where she'd dabbed it.

"Did you?" He was leaning in spite of his intention not to.

"I've learned a lot from you."

She was even using his technique of dodging questions.

When she did the thing with her hair, fluffing it so one strand got away from her and tickled his throat, he almost lost it. He wanted to run his hands down her sleek back and squeeze her adorable behind. He wanted to know if she wore sexy underwear or maybe none at all. Most of all, he wanted to kiss her senseless.

She backed off in the nick of time as far as his self-control was concerned. Where had she learned that kind of timing? He doubted whether it could be taught.

"I'm so sleepy," she said in a low voice. "Are you going to show up before my brunch date tomorrow?"

"No," he said crossly, feeling he'd somehow been had. His trick with the keys didn't seem so clever anymore.

Before he knew it, she had him out in the hallway, disgruntled and stiff from sleeping propped against her door.

Julie Myers still had a long way to go in the bad-girl department, but she was definitely showing some not-so-nice tendencies. Unfortunately he was on the receiving end, and she was making him hot and bothered.

Maybe it was time to rev up his own social life.

8

⟵⟶

"Who sent the basket of flowers?" Karen spotted the bouquet as soon as she came into Julie's apartment. "Nice! Do we ever have some catching up to do! I haven't seen you since girls' night out at the bowling alley."

"Peter sent them. Did you enjoy your two weeks in sunny Florida?"

"My stepfather was a jerk, as usual, but Mom and I had fun. I brought you some shells and sand dollars." She handed Julie a plastic bag of beach treasures and slipped out of her hot-pink parka. "You'll think of something clever to do with them."

"Great, thanks a lot."

"So what's happened since I left? I guess the date with Peter went well."

"He's nice. We had a good time."

"Have you gone out with him again?"

"One more time. He was out of town last weekend, but we're going to Club Now on Saturday night. There's some new alternative music group playing there. Guess he wants me to think he's with it."

"Sounds like fun. What about brunch with Peppermint Breath?"

"A disaster! He went ballistic because his bacon

wasn't crisp, then stiffed the waitress on the tip. I've had more fun digging out a splinter.''

"Now tell me about the hunk." Karen sat on the couch, folded her long legs encased in dove gray tights under her, looking ready for a long gab session.

"Hunk?"

Julie knew Karen wouldn't let her get away with playing dumb, but she didn't want to talk about Tom, not that there was anything to say. He'd called a few times to offer more dating advice, but she hadn't seen him since the first night she went out with Peter.

"Don't kid me. I saw him kiss you, and I've got a hundred or so witnesses. If someone kissed me like that—"

"You'd be embarrassed just like I was. So tell me what you did in Florida."

"Used up my hard-earned vacation time, got a tan and met lots of men—a few even had their original teeth and hair. To get back to the subject…"

"Peter is really nice. He's top salesperson at a real estate agency."

"Is he as tall as Tom?" Height was Karen's number one criteria.

"No, but tall enough for me."

"A shorty, huh? Forget him. What does Tom do when he's not setting fires at bowling lanes?"

"He owns an unfinished furniture store, but there's nothing between us, nothing at all."

"I saw your face after he kissed you. You were dewy-eyed! A goofy expression like that means you've just made love, or you'd like to."

"You're making that up!"

"We're best friends. I wouldn't kid you. Julie, you're twenty-five. It's time!"

"You weren't exactly walking on air when you had your affair with Howard."

"Howard was tall. That's all. You can't compare him to Tom. I saw the sparks between you two."

"Sparks as in sparkler. A flashy display signifying nothing."

Much as she'd missed Karen, Julie was glad when she left. For the first time in their long friendship, she didn't want to confide in her. It was hard enough admitting to herself what a stranglehold Tom had on her emotions. She'd lost a lot of sleep wishing he'd be the first man to make love to her, but it wasn't going to happen. Tom would never get romantically involved with a woman who wanted to get married. She'd known that even before he made it clear by his actions. Maybe he was a little bit attracted to her, but he wasn't going to do anything about it. He'd been avoiding her for two weeks.

She went over to the festive red, pink and white bouquet Peter had sent and buried her nose in a bright scarlet carnation. It was dyed and not very fragrant, but she should be thankful a man cared enough to send flowers. Maybe Peter wasn't as exciting or seductive as Tom, but he was considerate and nice, an unbeatable combination. Any woman would appreciate his attentions.

She ignored the tight feeling in her throat and rearranged the flowers to give the bouquet her own special flair. She had a date with Peter tomorrow night, and there was no reason why they wouldn't have fun together.

At nearly midnight on Friday, Tom decided he didn't care who won the hockey game he was watching on cable. He turned it off, went to the phone on his bedside stand, flipped through his worn leather address book, but it was too late to call anyone—even if there were anyone he wanted to call besides Julie. Even though he'd avoided seeing her since her date with Peter, she wasn't fading from his thoughts. In fact, his brief calls to her had given him a hollow, achy feeling. He was trying to help her be irresistible to other guys, but he was the one who couldn't stop thinking about her. He hadn't even followed through on his plans to jumpstart his own social life.

The phone rang as he was perched on the edge of the bed, staring dolefully at a well-thumbed page in his book. He was tempted to let the answering machine take it, but the strident rings penetrated his indifference. There was always that one chance in a thousand it was Julie with a report on a date or a need for advice.

He wished.

"Hi. If I owe you money, you're talking to an answering machine." Anyone who called at midnight deserved some lip, and he was in a crummy mood.

"Tom, hi! This is Monica Travis. Remember me?"

He drew a blank. "Ah…"

"We met at the Bowl-O-Rama."

"The twin." The bad-girl twin, he thought wryly.

"I know you and Julie are just friends, or I wouldn't dream of calling."

Sure she wouldn't.

"Tanya and I were going to Wisconsin to ski, but she has a terrible cold. I'm at loose ends, just sitting here in my little black teddy and fuzzy mules, wondering what to do this weekend." She sneezed into the mouthpiece.

"Maybe you'd better put your robe on," he advised, not especially enticed by her suggestive description.

"I know this is terribly pushy, but Tanya is so sick, and I've been dying to hear the Whiskey Flowers at Club Now."

"The Whiskey Flowers. Yeah, I've heard of them."

He'd already decided it was a bad idea to put his social life on hold any longer because of Julie. Monica was trying so hard, and she'd piqued his interest— sort of. Anyway, he had to start somewhere.

"I've heard they send shivers down your spine when they really get going,"

"Shivers, huh?" He'd gotten the same results with cold showers lately.

"The good part is, I have a friend who's tight with the club manager, and he gave me two good-anytime passes. But a girl can't go to Club Now alone without getting, you know, a reputation."

"A girl's reputation is important," he said with mock seriousness. She was fun to bait, if nothing else.

"Well, of course."

She was really purring, but he wasn't going to help her out. If she wanted him to go, she'd have to bring out her heavy artillery.

"I know this is terribly short notice for tomorrow night...."

Ouch! He remembered only too well what he'd told Julie. Accept no first dates after Thursday. She could ream him for the old double standard if he said yes to Monica tonight, but this was no big-deal date. If anything, it was therapeutic, a way to get Julie out of his head for a few hours.

Did that mean he was a superjerk for using someone he wasn't even sure he liked? Maybe, but she was the one who'd called him. Going out with her would be a diversion; it might even help his testosterone level to get back to normal. But when he thought of being with anyone but Julie, he felt as limp as last month's lettuce.

"It wouldn't be a date," Monica said, making her pitch. "Just two people with a mutual friend getting better acquainted."

She put more oomph into "getting better acquainted" than a stripper doing bumps and grinds on stage.

"If you'd like to," she added demurely.

"Sure, why not?" He felt more resigned than enthused.

"If you really want to…" She sounded teasingly petulant.

"Sounds like fun, Monica," he said in his best let's-party voice. "I'll pick you up. Where do you live?"

She gave him directions explicit enough to locate one bar out of hundreds on Chicago's south side, then signed off with belated breathiness.

He replaced the phone and stared glumly at the Michael Jordan poster on his bedroom wall. Well, he had a date. He had to start somewhere.

Monica's knack for giving directions came in handy Saturday night. Club Now was halfway to Iowa in a low-rent burb. From the outside it looked like a warehouse fallen on hard times. The inside was cavernous but short on decor. A huge tile dance floor had a small stage at one end with tiny tables crowded up to the edges and booths against the walls. Couples were already dancing, trailing powdery wax back to the sidelines.

"Isn't it adorable!" Monica trilled, looking sallow as yellow light beams from the ceiling washed over her face.

The beams turned to red, emphasizing her like-colored nose. She'd tried to hide it in the van coming over, but she was nursing a full-blown head cold, taking swigs from an over-the-counter cold medication whenever she thought he wasn't paying attention.

A female singer was wailing about love, betrayal and the man who'd done her wrong, while couples, a lot of them younger than him, struggled to find a dance step compatible with the gloomy lyrics.

Even in the anything-goes atmosphere, Monica's cutesy offbeat style looked out of place. Her white see-through lace bodysuit was too California chic for his taste, and she'd made it worse by wearing a black bra and bikinis under it. Her underwear was visible through strategically placed rips in her faded jeans. Her denim cap with a big starburst pin looked like a holdover from high school. He wasn't impressed, if that had been her intention.

He felt like a rogue bear coming out of hibernation—disgruntled and dissatisfied.

They found a booth, and Monica started to slide in across from him, then changed her mind after he was seated, crowding him against the poster-hung wall. They made small talk until a waitress in bike shorts and midriff-baring top bounded over to their table.

"This is still my treat," Monica said, then ordered a Japanese beer he'd never heard of. When they didn't have it, she pouted and settled for white wine.

"Anything on tap," he told the waitress, cutting off her lengthy recitation of the brands available.

Monica took another swig of cold medicine.

"Isn't this groovy?" she trilled.

"Are you sure that much medicine is good for you?" he asked, trying to ignore her choice of descriptive words.

"Oh, it's just my allergies acting up. No problem."

No problem, Tom thought, except he'd been dumb to agree to this date. He liked to make the first move, do the choosing.

Which had nothing whatsoever to do with his grouchy mood. He just didn't want to be here; he didn't want to be with anyone who wasn't Julie, but dating her wasn't an option.

It wasn't.

He glanced around, focusing on a familiar-looking couple who were searching for an unoccupied table on the opposite side of the club. They didn't have any success there, so they started walking across the floor, dodging dancers.

Tom stopped breathing for a minute, then nodded his head to acknowledge Peter's enthusiastic wave. Peter headed in their direction, Julie a step behind him.

Tom did a double take, silently applauding the way Julie looked in a really short black jumper with a white T-shirt under it. She was wearing black tights and flat heels that made her look small and delicate beside Peter.

Why the heck was Peter bringing her to his booth? If Julie were *his* date, he'd head for the nearest dark corner, pull her onto his lap, and—

Good ol' Peter turned on his best salesman's smile

and gave Tom the old-buddy greeting, barely giving Monica the once-over. He had to be really interested in his own date to overlook all that Monica was displaying under the lace.

"Do you mind if we join you?" Peter asked, gesturing for Julie to slide in across from Tom. She hesitated, seemed to look at Tom for advice, then slowly—and he thought reluctantly—seated herself across the scarred wooden table from him. The two women greeted each other and talked a little, but he was too befuddled to notice what they said.

"Let's dance," he said to Monica, refusing to meet Julie's eyes, afraid of what he'd see there even though he had a right to date anyone he wanted, her friend or not.

Why had he told Julie he wasn't interested in hitting on her friends? And why did it matter so much if Julie thought he was a double-crossing liar? Anyway, *he* hadn't initiated this date. It wasn't his fault Julie's friend was an aggressive bad girl.

The warm-up band stopped playing and got up for their break just as he and Monica found an open patch of floor to begin dancing. Piped-in music blared over the speaker system, and most couples started leaving the floor. Tom wanted to go back to the booth, too, but Monica insisted on dancing to the recorded music.

"Let's wait until the band comes back," he said, but Monica was already flailing around, arms beating the air while her hips gyrated like a spinning top. Men around them were not unaware. He was totally embarrassed, watching flat-footed without a clue how to join in on her whirling dervish routine.

After an endless period of slightly swaying in front of her, trying to talk her off the floor, Tom was ready to go home. She started coughing and headed back to the booth for her bottle of medicine, to where Julie sat with her date.

Julie sat back and watched while Peter made a ritual of ordering her mineral water and his imported beer from the waitress. Tom was squirming, and she was enjoying it. She knew Monica's dancing was a joke. If he wanted a graceful partner, he should have asked Tanya, the talented twin. Julie could have told him that.

But why would *he* ask *her* for advice?

"Excuse me a minute, honey," Peter said. "I'm trying to sell a town house to that couple over there. Can't hurt to let them see me here."

When had she become his "honey?" Tom and Monica were walking toward the booth, and she pretended to search for something in her purse to avoid looking at them.

"I have to visit the little girls' room," Monica announced, retrieving her purse and prancing off on too high heels that made her mostly exposed rear bounce from side to side.

If Tanya weren't such a sweetheart, Julie thought.

"She asked me out," Tom said sheepishly, sliding in across from her.

"Did she?" Julie put all the saccharine sweetness she could muster into her voice. "I talked to Tanya Thursday night, and the twins were planning to ski this weekend."

"Tanya has a bad cold."

"Then Monica asked you—"

"Friday night," he admitted glumly.

"So last-minute dates are okay for men. I'm never going to get all your rules sorted out."

"I should've said no." He frowned, pulling his brows closer together, making her want to trace them with the tips of her fingers.

She'd never seen a face quite like his. All his features were ordinary enough—maybe regular was more descriptive—but combined they added up to much more than an average-looking guy. She'd love to be a sculptor and choose him as her model. She could almost feel his masculine beauty taking form in wet clay under her fingers.

She was kidding herself. What she really wanted was to stroke his cheek, feel the whisper of his breath on her fingertips, press her lips against his lids—

She loved him. She couldn't deny the truth any longer.

"Your social life doesn't matter to me," she lied, wondering if her face had betrayed her. People in love had a special glow—but hopefully only when their feelings were reciprocated.

"The important thing," he said, blatantly changing the subject, "is how you're doing with Peter. Has he proposed yet?"

"Don't be silly. I hardly know him."

"Is there a certain timeline that has to be followed?"

She scowled at him.

"Sorry, I'm being facetious."

"I'll keep you posted," she said dryly.

He was tapping his fingers on the table, looking at his own hand instead of at her.

"Are you enjoying the games?" she asked.

"What games?"

"The Bulls. What games do you think I mean?"

"Yeah, of course, the Bulls. They won last week. Great game."

Most men would have launched into a play-by-play or at least a two-minute recap. He couldn't muster any excitement and went back to studying his knuckles.

This was getting harder every time he saw her, he thought grimly. The sooner she found Mr. Right, the better for him. She was really getting under his skin, and he didn't like it. He was imagining her in a see-through bodysuit like Monica's, only with a tiny white G-string and a bandage-size bra. Worse, there was nothing he'd like more than getting naked with her, but he'd been over that scene a few thousand times in his mind. It wasn't going to happen.

"Well, I'm glad they're having a good season," she said.

Was she reminding him that he still owed her something for the tickets? No, that wasn't Julie's style. She'd let him off the hook, and she wouldn't dangle an obligation over his head. No wonder he liked her so much.

That was it! He did like her—immensely. It was a new experience for him to so enthusiastically like a woman. So far he hadn't found a single thing about Julie that didn't please him.

He didn't just like the way she looked, he liked everything: her warmth, her sense of humor, her honesty.

"Why are you grinning?" she asked.

"I didn't know I was."

"You must be amused about something."

"Not exactly."

How could he explain? There was no way to tell a woman he liked her without sounding like a guy who wanted to break up. Not that she was his to dump.

He made the mistake of looking up and meeting her eyes, knowing he could get lost in those shimmering blue depths. He wanted to tickle her forehead by blowing on her bangs; he wanted to nuzzle her nose and inhale the fragrance of her skin.

If he didn't stop thinking this way, he was going to jump across the table that separated them. She should be with him, not Carlyle.

"Julie…"

"Tom…"

Say something to break this tension, he wanted to shout, but all she did was repeat his name. "Tom."

She reached across the table and lightly stroked his closed fist, her neat pink nails sending little tremors up his arm.

"Monica asked me to come here with her. It was a mistake."

"I know about mistakes."

She sounded sad, and he wanted her to be happy.

"Don't do it anymore," he said.

"Do what?" She jerked her hand away as though he'd slapped it.

"Don't try to be a bad girl. Any guy who doesn't appreciate you the way you are doesn't deserve you."

Her laugh was a soft tinkle that reverberated down his spine.

"I'm hopeless at being anyone but me."

"That's not a bad thing. You're beautiful, sweet…"

"Sorry I took so long," Peter said, returning to the booth. "They had a lot of questions about financing."

''That's okay,'' Julie said. ''You're just in time for the big performance.''

Tom felt nauseated when Peter started massaging her arm. Fortunately the Whiskey Flowers arrived, distracting all three of them. Five fair-haired, emaciated female musicians were shuffling around the stage, getting ready to do their stuff, whatever that was.

Julie laughed, apparently entertained by some corny remark of Peter's. There was nothing wrong with her technique. Carlyle was puffed up like a peacock when the peahens were in heat.

Listening to a post-date report wasn't too bad, but he never wanted to be an on-the-spot observer again. It was all he could do to keep from booting Peter across the floor and out the door.

Monica finally came back, wineglasses in both hands.

''That cute blond bartender insisted on giving me two for one,'' she said, giggling. She sipped from one, and spilled part of the other when she sneezed violently.

''If you're not feeling well, maybe we should go,'' Tom suggested.

''I'll be fine, but I never did get to the little girls' room.''

She tottered off, apparently forgetting she was dying to hear the Whiskey Flowers. The band bombarded the room with a drumroll that hurt his ears, then launched into a number that seemed to combine music and mayhem.

Peter insisted on joining the dancers who were stomping around to the beat. Julie gave Tom a look

that could have meant "Save me!" But it probably
didn't, so he sat alone, nursing a warm beer, watching
Julie shake her gorgeous little behind, and brooding
over her budding relationship with Carlyle.

What was this, the third date? He tried to figure
out Peter's routine. Hand holding and a peck on the
first date; some kissy-kissy and a feel or two on the
second. Would he make a big move tonight, or wait
until date four?

Julie was really on the wrong track, but what could
he do about it?

Monica didn't come back—no loss to him—but it
forced him to watch Julie dancing, Julie smiling at
Peter, Julie laughing. The set finally ended, and they
came back to the booth. The recorded music grated
on his nerves, but not as much as Peter bragging to
Julie about all the big sales he'd made.

He'd had enough of this impromptu Double Date
from Hell. He stood and spotted Monica draped over
the bar, flirting with a muscle-bound bartender. He
mumbled good-night and went to fetch his so-called
date.

"Let's go, Monica."

"Are you kidding? The party is just warming up."
Her eyes were unfocused; the bottle of cold medication sitting in front of her was nearly empty.

"I'm going. You should come with me."

"You're not as much fun as I thought you'd be,"
she accused him. "I want to have some fun tonight."

"Fine, but I'm leaving. If you're coming, let's go."

"No way."

He debated whether to make a scene hauling her
out of there and decided against it. He wasn't going

to fight a steely eyed bartender over a woman who was old enough to take care of herself.

He experienced a pang of conscience as he claimed his coat, then left the overheated, under-ventilated building, sucking in fresh, frigid air like a man on a respirator. He was unlocking the van when Julie caught up with him.

"You can't just leave Monica here!" she said angrily.

"Why not? She refuses to leave with me, and it appears she won't have any trouble getting a ride home."

The look Julie gave him was withering, and he knew she was right. He'd brought Monica here, and any woman with half a brain went home with the guy who brought her out, but if she didn't want to....

"She's zonked out on cold medicine, not drunk, if that's what you think," Julie said.

"I think it's a combination of both. If you're so worried about her, you and Peter take her home."

He was in the wrong, but he was too damn stubborn to go back into that bedlam after Monica when the woman who was making him crazy was standing right in front of him.

"No way. You brought her. She's your responsibility."

"All right, then you ride with me to take care of her."

"That is so unfair!" Julie sputtered, but she could see Tom's point. Who knew what Monica, her soon-to-be-ex-friend, would pull with her wits dulled by a whole bottle of medicine and wine chasers.

She led the way back inside, in a quandary because

there was no way to win. Tom was already mad because she'd foiled his getaway. Peter wasn't going to jump for joy if he got saddled with Monica.

It took the three of them to persuade Monica to leave, and she probably only went because the bartender-of-the-hour was hitting on a redhead at the other end of the bar.

"I don't want her getting sick in my car," Peter groused when they finally got her out to the parking lot.

"I'm not riding alone with her," Tom insisted. "She's your friend."

Men! Julie wanted to bang their heads together.

"I'll ride with Tom and Monica," she said, not as reluctant as she pretended.

"I don't think Brunswick needs protecting," Peter complained.

"I'm worried about her," Julie insisted. "Who knows what was in that medicine? I'd better go with her."

"Well, I'll follow, then take you home," Peter said, obviously unwilling to leave his date with Tom.

Monica giggled when Tom fastened the seat belt across her lap on the passenger side where Julie insisted she sit. She giggled all the way to the expressway with Julie sitting in the seat behind her.

"Hospital or home?" Tom asked dryly.

"Home, I think. Then Tanya can decide."

Thankfully, Monica was snoring loudly after a few minutes. Julie could see Peter's lights right on their tail. Did he think she was being kidnapped?

"So how was your date?" Tom asked after a long silence.

''Splendid.'' If he didn't recognize sarcasm when he heard it, he could believe whatever he liked.

They rode the rest of the way in silence.

Monica woke up when they got to the twins' apartment, fortunately on the ground floor. Either she really was woozy, or she'd missed her calling. She gave a performance Hollywood's best couldn't top, demanding that two strong men help her inside, her arms draped around their shoulders and her feet dragging. At the door she launched into an apology heavily laced with excuses and ended with a threat to sue the company that made the cold medication.

''You should have followed the directions,'' Tom noted pointedly.

Peter only grunted. Monica had some pounds packed into her peekaboo bodysuit.

They left her with a red-nosed and very angry twin.

''Night,'' Tom said curtly to Julie, as if it were her fault that Monica had been so eager to keep their date she'd taken too much medicine.

Peter took Julie home, complaining most of the way. At least now she knew why he was a good prospect for an engagement but a poor risk for the long haul. Before they got to her place, he'd outlined a theory to explain Monica's behavior that made the JFK conspiracy ones look like kids' play.

''Good night,'' he grunted when they'd reached her apartment building, leaving her at the outside door without getting out of his car.

What a night! Julie couldn't wait to get to bed, but when she finally did, her mind wouldn't turn off. She tossed, turned and had a pillow fight—with her pillow. She was going crazy! Why couldn't that dumb lug see that the Monicas of the world weren't for him?

If Tom wanted a bad girl, she could be one. For him. Not for anyone else.

Would he ever give her a chance?

9

"What's going on with you?" Tina challenged.

"You coerced me into kitchen duty, that's what's going on with me," Tom said, trying to fit the last leftovers into his parents' refrigerator.

"You don't want Mom cleaning up her own birthday dinner, do you?"

"No, but why not use your own domestic help instead of me?"

"Dan's been looking forward to the hockey game all week."

"Of course, I hate sports," he said sarcastically.

"I haven't had a chance to really talk to you since the wedding," his twin said. "Something's bugging you."

He wasn't in the mood to be analyzed, especially not by his sister. She knew him too well.

"Yeah, I've got five bucks on the Red Wings, and I'm missing the game."

"You're not yourself," she said thoughtfully. "Does it have something to do with Julie Myers?"

"No."

He denied it too quickly and too vehemently. Tina wasn't going to get off his case.

"Why is she dating Peter if you're interested? I can't believe she dumped you."

"She didn't dump me because we were never a couple." He slammed the door of the fridge, rattling the ceramic clown cookie jar sitting on top.

"If you're hung up on her—"

"I'm not! She's not my type."

"Your type!" She laughed and swatted him across the shoulders with a dish towel. "Your type is any female with breasts."

"You know, you're really annoying since you got married."

"I was really annoying before I got married. Seriously, Tom, I like Julie. Maybe it's time to give up on bimbos."

"Maybe it's time for you to mind your own business."

"You are touchy. And not very happy, I think."

"Look, Tina—"

"We used to talk about everything," she said glumly.

"Don't get your feelings hurt. There's nothing to talk about."

"I heard through the grapevine Peter likes Julie a lot, but he's not sure yet whether she has that special something…"

"Carlyle wouldn't know special if it came up and bit him on the butt."

"So, it is that way," his sister said.

He hated it when she got that wise, all-knowing look, mainly because it usually meant she was right.

"Drop it." He slammed a cupboard door shut, this time unintentionally.

"Maybe it's time for you to grow up," she said without rancor.

"I've got to go."

"You're angry."

"No."

He wasn't mad, but he didn't have words to tell his sister how he felt about Julie. Not even Tina would understand his need to stay unattached. Most women were born matchmakers. They saw single men as loose cannons, dangerous until they were tied down and brought under control.

But, damn, he wished Julie would find someone better than Peter. Sure, he was a decent guy—for a jerk. He had a good job and seemed to like her, but was he the best she could do?

Instead of going home he went to a mall and played arcade games until he noticed he was the only guy in the place old enough to shave. He left the arcade with its flashy graphics and simulated sounds. Tina's remark about growing up still stung, but it was Julie who was turning his life upside down.

If Peter was the man she wanted, he'd just have to live with it. True, she'd had a few other dates in the past couple of weeks but none that developed into anything. Maybe it was time to find out how much she cared about Peter—and do something to move their relationship along. He was living in limbo, and the only way to get back to normal was to know she was paired up. She was inside his head, but he wasn't a one-woman man. Definitely not. Definitely…

Peter! He could grow to loathe the little twerp, but jealousy wasn't his style. He wouldn't let himself think about Carlyle's stubby fingers and sloppy lips roaming over Julie's satiny skin. If he wanted to preserve his life-style, he had to get Peter and Julie committed to each other. Then he wouldn't have an excuse to see her again, and what he was feeling now would be history.

Without conscious thought, he found himself on Higgins Road headed toward Julie's place. Where did he think he was going?

He made an abrupt right turn and slowed to a crawl, struck by an uncomfortable thought. Maybe his advice was the problem. Carlyle wanted a nice girl to marry, and he'd been teaching Julie how to be a bad girl. It was possible—even probable—his advice had backfired.

He was worse than Dr. Frankenstein. He'd taken a beautiful, sweet woman and tried to turn her into a cheap, phony, party girl. No wonder Peter had doubts about her.

Now that he'd accepted responsibility, he knew what he had to do.

When the phone rang, Julie hoped it was her mother or her grandmother in Peoria or even a telemarketer—anyone who didn't know about Tom. She was in love and didn't want to be. How long was it going to take to get over Brunswick? She picked the receiver up reluctantly and said hello.

"Julie, it's Tom. Can I come over and talk to you?"

"You're asking to come over?"

She was amazed. It was Tom's style to drop in anytime he felt like it and ruin her day by reminding her he was unavailable. As much as she wanted to be with him, it was just too painful to go on with the teacher-pupil charade.

"If you don't mind? I think you should try a new approach."

"What approach?"

"It's complicated. I'd rather explain in person."

She could feel her heart pounding in her chest. She didn't want him in her apartment. He always seemed to dwarf the small living room and cut off her oxygen supply. And there was always the danger that he'd... That she'd...

"Don't come here," she gasped. "I'll meet you at the bagel shop on Hoover, the one next to the Video Mart."

"I know the place. Is twenty minutes too soon?"

Twenty years were too soon if he intended to give her more advice on hooking a man, but she mumbled her assent.

The shop was nearly empty; they closed early on Sunday. Tom was already seated at a small table by the window, idly breaking apart a cinnamon-raisin bagel he'd bought, apparently to justify using the table. He didn't seem to be eating it.

He stood and pulled out a chair for her when she approached.

"Can I get something for you?"

He hadn't touched his coffee.

"No, thank you."

He launched right into his pitch. She had the uncomfortable feeling he'd been rehearsing it in his mind.

"Something's going wrong," he said, holding a section of bagel so tightly it crumbled and fell out of his fingers.

"Tom, you don't need to—"

"Yes, I do."

How was he going to explain? He could try the direct approach. *Julie, I've given you stupid advice.* Or maybe subtlety would work. *Julie, there's more than one way to skin a skunk.*

Corny, corny, corny!

"What I think is…" he began.

The trouble was, he couldn't think straight with Julie across from him, her cheeks tinged with pink and her lips slightly parted, revealing the polished white of her pretty teeth. She was fantastic as she was, in her own special way, and he'd been an arrogant fool to try to change her.

"I thought we could go on a date."

He astonished himself even more than her, but it made sense. Pretend they were strangers on a blind date and convince her the real Julie was far more appealing than any bad girl.

"Let's act as though we've been set up on a blind date," he started to explain. "I'll react the way I would at a real first meeting. You can be totally un-inhibited with me, so we can figure out what works and what doesn't."

"Uninhibited?" She looked skeptical. "I don't see the point."

She didn't know what to do. Men weren't exactly dropping like flies at her feet, but she wasn't unhappy with her progress—only with the way she felt about Tom. Was he still determined to turn her into a femme fatale? More importantly, why?

"Indulge me," he said.

He smiled a little sheepishly, but to her it was like a million candles glowing just for her. Common sense warned her to say no to his wacky plan; she didn't need more frustration in her life, but she did need Tom. If one date was his best offer, she wasn't strong enough to refuse.

"Okay."

She smiled, but her heart was aching. When she'd asked for his help, she'd naively believed he could never mean anything to her. Men like him were never interested in nice girls like her. Knowing his attitude about marriage should have made her immune to him.

How could she be so wrong? She was head-over-heels in love with Tom, but she didn't know how to tell him she'd lost interest in finding a husband. She wanted to be with him, even if it meant living day to day with no hope of permanent commitment.

"Tomorrow okay?" he asked.

"A Monday date? Of course, it isn't a real date, is it? Tomorrow will work."

He looked relieved. "We'll figure out what it will take to get Peter to pop the question."

Peter was the wrong popper! She didn't want a proposal, only a real first date with Tom.

"I'll pick you up at eight, if that's okay?"

"Yes."

"Just be yourself," he said as she stood to leave.

She didn't understand why he said that, but this wasn't the time or the place to go into it. She wanted to get away before she did something really dumb—like tell him how she felt.

What happened to being an alluring, mysterious creature? she wondered on the way home. Was this date going to be her final exam from Professor Tom? If so, she had a feeling she was in for a flunking grade.

* * *

She could hardly concentrate on work all the next day. Monday was laundry night, bill-paying night, clean-the-bathroom night. No one had a *real* date on Monday, so she could only believe Tom wanted to get their lessons over with.

By the time he buzzed her, Julie was determined to show him what she'd learned over the past month. She was doubly determined not to let him know how she felt about him.

"Hi, I'm Tom."

"I'm Julie, your blind date," she said, throwing herself into the role-playing.

"You look gorgeous."

"Thank you. So do you. I love turtlenecks."

She'd never seen him look better. He was wearing a brown herringbone sport coat over dark brown pleated trousers and matching knit shirt. He'd gotten a haircut, not short but stylish, and fragrant aftershave wafted around his freshly shaved face.

"Here, let me fix this," she said.

Playing bad girl to the hilt, she reached up and pretended to adjust the fold in his collar, letting her fingers graze the underside of his chin.

"There, that looks wonderful."

She handed him her coat and backed into him when he helped her with it. On the way downstairs she tucked her hand into the crook of his arm so they had to walk side by side, crowded close together.

He drove to a steak house less than twenty minutes away, not her idea of a romantic setting, but it wouldn't be crowded on a Monday night.

"They specialize in rare and juicy beef, but there's a good choice of other things," he said.

She trilled and made a suggestive comment about steak building hormone levels. She didn't know her score so far, but she was putting all she had into it, laughing at his jokes whether they were funny or not, inching as close as possible, leaving her coat unbuttoned to reveal lots of thigh under her Black Watch plaid miniskirt. As a kicker, she was wearing the patent-leather spikes she'd bought on a dare in high school. They pinched her toes but did wonderful things for her ankles.

At the restaurant they were led to a high-backed wooden booth with burgundy leather seats, and she remembered to smooth her sweater as she was sitting down across from him. She preferred to wear a tailored white blouse with her plaid skirt, but the sweater was a flattering pink shade with short sleeves and a tendency to cling where it could do a bad girl the most good.

"Are you a big steak eater?" she asked, remembering she wasn't supposed to know a thing about her "blind" date.

"I guess." He was studying the menu, not giving her any help or encouragement. Was he testing her aggressiveness by sitting there like an impenetrable wall?

She struggled to keep the conversation going without much help from him. If she didn't rate an A in small talk and senseless chatter, she'd like to see him try flirting with the Sphinx.

Desperate to get some reaction from him, she found his leg under the table and rubbed her calf against his. If this didn't thaw him...

She slipped one shoe off and let her toe crawl up his leg.

"That's enough," he said. "Here's our waiter."

"Hi, I'm Todd. I'll be your server tonight."

She let Tom order for her, grateful when he suggested scallops instead of half a cow. She didn't really like the Manhattan she ordered, but it sounded sophisticated.

What more can I do? she wondered. She wanted to scream or jump up and down, anything to knock the bland, slightly bored expression off his face.

The place was more than half-empty; they had a semidark corner all to themselves. When Todd the Server brought their salads and disappeared, she decided to knock the socks off her stone-faced date.

Her shoe was still off; both were, for the sake of her toes. She leaned forward, keeping up a meaningless spiel about the kind of flowers men ordered at the shop for their girlfriends. Mustering all her courage, she lifted one leg and let her toes come to rest squarely on target.

Tom was shocked! And more! Her busy little toes burrowed against his crotch, causing more havoc than she could imagine. In self-defense, he caught her foot and moved it away, but not before he'd hardened so obviously he had to fan his napkin over his lap.

"Eat your salad." It was probably the dumbest thing he'd ever said.

He blamed himself. She was pretending to be shallow and vacuous, flattering him and flirting, pushing the envelope, throwing in some outrageous conduct to let him know she was available.

He'd coached her well, but he wasn't at all proud of it. He dated the women she was emulating all the time, and most of them went on to other guys with few regrets when he dumped them. He was the love-

'em-and-leave-'em type, and he always picked women who were easy to forget.

If any woman but Julie had pulled the toe trick on him, he would have taken it as an invitation and enjoyed the rest of the evening immensely. But he'd taken a girl who was perfect—sweet, charming, lovely, innocent—and taught her nothing but cheap tricks she didn't need.

He was too ashamed to look her in the eyes.

"Do I get an A, Professor?" she asked, not quite able to conceal her embarrassment.

"That wasn't nice, Julie."

Who was he to reprimand her? He was utterly disgusted with himself.

"I'm sorry." She pushed a crouton around on her salad and looked as unhappy as he felt.

"No, it's my fault. Everything I've told you about the bad-girl rules is bull. The only guy you'll catch with cheap tricks is a jerk like me. Forget everything I've told you, Julie. Please. You were perfect just the way you were."

"I don't understand."

She looked stricken. He couldn't feel worse if he'd slapped her.

"Yes, you do. You're a sweet, loving person, and I've tried to make you into a clone of your friend Monica. Forget everything I've told you."

"But your rules seem to work."

He wanted to kiss away the hurt and confusion on her face, but anything he did now would only make it worse.

"No, you've made a hit with Peter in spite of what I've told you, and even he has some doubts. Look, I'll give you back the tickets I haven't used. Take

Peter. Take anyone you like. You don't need my advice, and you never did. Brad was stupid. Worse than stupid. He passed up the chance for a solid-gold relationship, and you absolutely should not change because of a bad experience with him. You were perfect just the way you were.''

Her jaw fell open; she was beyond words. Tom's speech had been overwhelming, and she could tell he was angry at himself, not her.

''That's why I brought you here tonight—to tell you that,'' he said glumly.

''Tom, I don't think I can eat anything. I'm sorry, especially for—you know.''

''You got that part just right.'' He grinned ruefully. ''I'm not quite ready to leave.''

''I'll stay if you'll forget about giving back the tickets. You don't owe me anything.''

''Thanks.'' He wasn't thanking her for the tickets, only for being the kind of person she was. ''I guess this is where I ask if we can still be friends.''

What was he doing? He wasn't sure himself. He should stop seeing her or go for a long swim in the Big Lake, but he wasn't ready to jump into Lake Michigan—or stop seeing her. He wasn't ready to push her out of his life, at least not until she found someone who was right for her. He still owed her that; he owed it to himself. He wouldn't get any rest—and he might never have a social life again—until she was securely attached to someone else. And he wasn't entirely convinced that would make him happy, either.

Surprisingly, the rest of the evening was really fun, for him at least. They talked about themselves, not her dates, not his dates, not rules for dates. He told her how he'd started the store; she shared her ambition to open her own flower shop, with money her grandfather had left her, when she had enough experience. They both loved board games and ethnic festivals. He liked her; he liked her an awful lot. And that scared him.

Outside the evening was overcast but mild with hardly any wind; it boded well for an early spring. When he walked her to the outer door of her complex, it was nearly midnight.

"Can I come up?" he asked, following her into the vestibule.

"Sorry, not on the first date."

She was having fun with him, and it was more erotic than her toes caressing his crotch.

"For a few minutes?" Being turned down always challenged him, but this was different. He wanted to be with her awhile longer on any terms.

"No, I don't think so." She was wavering.

"Can I kiss you good-night?"

The devil made him ask—or maybe it was because he could still remember the feel of her foot burrowing against him.

"Maybe a little peck on the cheek," she said, pointing somewhere in the vicinity of her chin and mouth.

She was playing with fire and could only get hurt, Tom knew, but it was hard to worry when she was driving him crazy. He wanted her in his arms, in his bed.

He bent his head and gently let his lips tease the corner of her mouth, nibbling a little as he eased his arms around her. Her coat was swinging open, and her breasts pressed against him, firm and delectable under the downy sweater. He was stunned by his own reaction; he hadn't even kissed her properly, and he was hard and throbbing. He tried to blame it on his celibate life-style of late, but knew it was Julie. All Julie.

She raised her arm and circled his neck, gloved fingers stroking the skin under his collar. He couldn't take any more. He kissed her hard and long, parting her lips with his tongue and forcefully taking what he wanted, holding her head in his hands and not sparing himself or her.

It was no first-date kiss; he was going too far too fast, so eager for the sweetness of her mouth, he forgot himself.

Using all the self-control he possessed, he backed off for an instant, giving her a chance to protest or leave. Instead she pulled his head down, pressing her pelvis against him, weakening all his resolve in the sheer torturous pleasure of holding her close. He slid her coat off her shoulders and ran his hands down her back, gripping her buttocks, squeezing and pulling her even closer until he was almost lifting her off the floor.

The tiny vestibule was steamy warm, and he heard her gasping for air even as his own lungs panted for oxygen. He didn't know how they'd come so far so fast. It was a fantasy come to life—Julie locked against him, riding his knee between her thighs as he tried to clear his head and still not lose what was happening.

"Maybe you could come up for a few minutes," she said, no artifice in her husky whisper.

He kissed her gently, drawing her tongue into his mouth but dropping his hands and knee. This wasn't just sex. It was— He didn't know. Whatever was happening, he wanted it to go on forever. The wildest and best sex he'd ever had was nothing compared to Julie's mouth on his. He ached to be inside her, but a warm, quiet joy beyond his experience was overpowering him. He could hardly breathe; his knees were trembling.

He couldn't go up to her place. She wouldn't resist, but he couldn't make love to her, not knowing as he did all the connotations it would have for her—and maybe for him, too.

How could he be so happy and so miserable?

The first time he'd run a four-minute mile, he had the flu. He'd been terrified every step, afraid he'd get sick in front of the crowd at the track meet, afraid he'd disgrace himself and fail his team. He'd exerted himself to the max, his feet sprouting wings because he was desperate.

That race was nothing compared to the effort it took to pull away from Julie.

"I can't," he said.

She looked stricken and said something—thanked him for the dinner, maybe—but he was backing away in a daze, grappling with the door handle, stepping out into cooler air that beaded the sweat on his forehead.

He couldn't have a casual fling with Julie. He had to stop seeing her. His hormones—and his heart—were going haywire. If he could just have sex with her—get her out of his system...

No, that wasn't the answer.

He walked over to the van, knowing he could have enticed her to do anything, everything. She wanted him as badly as he wanted her.

He started the engine and backed up, afraid he'd

shrivel up and die if he didn't make love to her. It wasn't too late to go back.

He stopped at the exit, still too shaken to drive and aching to go back to her.

Just once. If he could make love to her just once, it might break the spell she had on him. He could get back to normal; he could feel like a separate individual again, his life unfettered by an overwhelming need for her.

"Don't kid yourself," he said out loud.

Once wouldn't be enough, not with Julie. She'd gotten under his skin and into his heart. He wanted her in bed and out of it, but he couldn't accept her yours-forever terms.

He had to end it.

He had to stop pretending there was nothing between them to end.

Tomorrow he'd say goodbye for good.

He had to.

10

Could Tom kiss her the way he had and not call?

Julie fumbled her way through Tuesday, scarcely able to count out a dozen roses without pricking her finger or tipping over a vase. She was in a continual state of agitation, hoping to look up and see Tom every time the door opened.

After work she rushed home, not even stopping to pick up her cleaning.

Should she call him? His latest advice was to be herself, and the real Julie Myers was much too chicken to call a man and tell him she was crazy about him. But how would he know if she didn't tell him? Tom still thought she was totally focused on marriage, and she knew he wanted no part of that.

Last night he'd wanted her, though, and her whole body had been fine-tuned to respond. They'd been so close she could still feel the sparks when she closed her eyes. What Tom didn't want was commitment, and he had no way of knowing she'd settle for anything he was willing to give.

Forget wedding invitations! She'd already picked them out with the wrong man. How could she tell Tom he was the right one without sending him running in the opposite direction? They didn't have to shop for rings; she'd settle for holding hands at the movie on a real date or calling each other just to talk.

Her answering machine was blinking when she came in the door. She so desperately wanted it to be Tom, she was afraid to hear the message.

She took off her coat and dropped it on the couch, steeling herself for the disappointment of hearing any voice but Tom's. She pushed the play button.

It was Tom. She wanted to hug someone, but a throw pillow from the couch had to do.

"You did great last night," his recorded voice said.

Something in his tone made her think of a teacher handing out a passing grade. This wasn't at all what she wanted to hear.

"...Training completed...not another thing I can teach you. Good luck with Peter or whoever. Maybe I'll see you around sometime."

How could he leave a message like that on her machine? She thought her heart would shatter into a trillion pieces. How could he kiss her for real, then be so cavalier in dismissing her from his life?

For several long minutes she stood rooted to the spot, more stunned than angry. It wasn't as though he'd jilted her. They'd never even been on a real date. All he'd promised to do was help her look for Mr. Right. It was her bad fortune to fall madly in love with Mr. Not Interested.

"I don't understand," she said out loud, torturing herself by replaying his message.

Last night he'd wanted to make love to her; she didn't need lessons to be sure of that. He probably thought he was being noble, turning his back on what they both wanted. Now it was too late to let him know she wasn't obsessed with marriage anymore.

She never would be a bad girl. And Tom had told her to just be herself. Did that mean she'd never make love with a man she truly loved?

Ignoring the hot tears trickling down her cheeks, she promised herself one thing. If she ever got the chance, she was going to experience everything a woman should. Tom was her second big disappointment, and this time it was her heart that was damaged, not her pride.

"And you, Tom Brunswick, can't tell a volcano from a mud pie!" she said, getting angrier by the minute because he was turning his back on what could be a wonderful relationship. She might never be bad, but she was sure she could be very, very good.

Peter called on Thursday to tell her he had to teach a real estate seminar in Milwaukee and wouldn't be available that weekend. She didn't know whether to be relieved or disappointed. Since Tom had bowed out of her life, she was mostly numb.

"That's the bad news," Peter said enthusiastically. "The good news is, I made top salesman for three months running, so I get a free weekend in Las Vegas."

"Congratulations. That's really nice, Peter."

"There's more. It's a trip for two. How about coming with me?"

"I don't know…"

"Shows, gambling, the high life. It'll be great."

"I'm not—"

"Don't turn it down right off. There're no strings attached. Separate rooms, if you want them. Honestly."

When she finally hung up, she had to admit Peter

was a very good salesperson. She hadn't said yes, but he'd convinced her to give it more thought. And darn, she did like the guy. They had fun together. It wasn't his fault he wasn't Tom.

Tom's March Madness Sale was in full swing, and business was good enough to hire another part-time person. He even had a shop-late week, staying open until ten every night. He worked the extra hours himself, too tired to do anything but drop into bed at the end of twelve- and fourteen-hour days. It was better than moping around his apartment missing Julie.

He'd picked up the phone to call her a dozen times in the past three weeks, but what could he say? He'd done the right thing—even if he'd done it the cowardly way with a message on her machine.

He'd be okay when the hollow ache went away. Maybe someday he'd even go to the bother of lining up a date with a wicked woman, preferably one who'd soured on the marriage scenario.

Meanwhile, he couldn't risk seeing Julie again—or even talking to her on the phone. He had the unfortunate habit, where she was concerned, of opening his mouth when his brain was on hold.

He made a special point of avoiding Dan and his annoying progress reports on how good ol' Peter was making out with Julie.

Tom was alone in the front of the store when the door opened. Turning to greet a customer, he watched his twin striding toward him.

Tina looked too much like him to be a beauty, but he had to admit marriage seemed to agree with her. Unlike his winter-dulled dark blond hair, hers was newly highlighted with gold. When he looked in the mirror, he saw lackluster brown eyes with fatigue shadows. Hers had sparkle.

"Hi, babe. You're lookin' good. A little bottom-heavy, but some guys like that."

"If you ever said anything nice without qualifying it—"

"Just kidding. What brings you here? Mom only worked until two."

"I didn't come to see her."

"That's ominous."

"I wanted to corner you in person since you seem to be exhibiting antisocial tendencies."

"It's called working hard."

"You're no workaholic. I've never known you not to find time for recreation."

He shrugged, not bothering to argue with a woman who'd shared his bathwater—more than a quarter century ago.

"Dan and I are giving a party Saturday. We'd like to have you come."

"Big party?"

"As many as our apartment will hold. Some of my friends have a Chicago layover this weekend."

"Not…ah—"

"Brenda? No. You didn't make much of a hit with her."

He could understand that. "And Julie, will she be there?"

"I didn't ask her. Can we count on you?"

"Sure, why not." He had to get back into circulation sometime, and Tina's friends were the perfect opportunity. "I'll bring some beer and chips."

"Come around eight. Dan will be glad to see you."

"The caged lion remembering his days in the wild?"

"You'll get your tail caught in a trap someday."

She left. He hated that she always got the last word.

Tina and Dan had an apartment in a huge complex. It was on the ground floor, pretty roomy and crowded with standing-room-only guests when he got there shortly after nine. He left two big bags of beer and chips in the kitchen, dropped his jacket with dozens of others on the honeymoon bed and went to join the party.

He had his choice of blondes, brunettes, even a bright-orange redhead, and most of the people there didn't seem to be couples. He was going to have a good time if it killed him. In fact, it was good to be back in circulation.

He targeted the redhead because he liked her shiny blue miniskirt and tight-fitting sweater. He was gradually working his way toward her when he saw Julie—with Peter's arm draped possessively across her shoulders.

He veered away before he was forced to say hello to them and found his sister in the kitchen uncovering a tray of crackers piled high with green and pink stuff.

"What's she doing here? You said you didn't invite her!" he accused Tina.

"Who?"

"You know damn well who! Julie!"

"I didn't invite her. I guess Dan invited Peter, and he brought her with him. They're pretty much a couple now, in case you didn't know."

"Great, I'm happy for her. It's exactly what she

wants.'' His tongue felt thick, and he hadn't even had a beer yet.

''I don't know.'' Tina whipped off a sheet of plastic wrap and handed him a tray of cheesy blobs. ''Pass these, would you?''

''What do you mean, you don't know?''

''Watching them together—Julie and Peter—I don't think the chemistry is right.''

''Next you'll tell me their vibes don't vibrate. Be serious! You're no matchmaker.''

''No, but I've seen enough of Julie to wonder.''

''Wonder what?''

''Whether she's interested in someone else.''

''Yeah, probably her dorky ex-fiancé.''

''No, I don't think he's in the picture anymore.''

''Next you'll tell me it's your feminine intuition.'' He laughed, but it came out as a snort.

''We'll see.''

Tom passed the sticky-looking tidbits, chatted up the redhead and managed to avoid Julie.

Tina, unfortunately, had a voice that could reach the tail section of a 747 from the cockpit. He couldn't help hearing what she said when she cornered Carlyle.

''Would you be a darling, Peter, and run to the Mini-Mart for some ice?'' She cajoled him in the tone she'd perfected on passengers who thought the two-drink limit should only apply to the pilot.

''You don't need to leave the party. I'll only be a few minutes,'' Peter said magnanimously when Julie offered to ride along with him.

Julie's heart had skipped a beat when she'd first seen Tom. Now Peter had made it practically impossible to avoid him. She must have been crazy to come to his sister's party, but she couldn't let him dictate where she went or who she saw—not anymore, she couldn't.

She looked around frantically, hoping to see a familiar face other than Tom's. Tina and Dan were busy hosting, and she didn't see any alternative except to escape to the bathroom. It was horrible feeling like a love-struck teenager, tormented by physical longing even in the midst of a crowd. She wanted to spend every waking and sleeping moment with Tom, but she didn't want to talk to him.

Coward! she accused herself. That was just what Tom would expect her to do: run and hide.

She never should have come, but Peter had been insistent. She was teetering on the brink of getting serious with him, but an inner voice kept cautioning her. Peter was sweet, attentive and not bad-looking; he was a genuinely nice man, but all she thought about was bad-boy Tom.

She took a deep breath, straightened her spine and mentally erased all Tom's rules about playing hard to get. She had to put the ball in his court again. If he let her go again, she'd have to stop yearning for him and give Peter a fair chance.

Peter was pressing her for an answer about the Vegas weekend. He had to use it within three months, and he kept promising separate rooms. She believed him, even though she could almost hear Tom lecturing her about being gullible. *If all he wanted was to gamble and see some shows, he could invite a buddy.*

Maybe Peter would expect more, but wasn't that her goal, to become an experienced woman?

A good girl would say no to the trip; a bad girl would go. Julie didn't know which she was anymore, thanks to her confusing tutor. She still blushed when she thought of her toes teasing and caressing his groin, all the more so because she could swear he'd gotten bigger.

Tom had created this dilemma. It was his fault she even knew Peter, and he was the one who'd coached her into being more desirable to him. She couldn't make up her mind about Vegas, so why not ask her former tutor? Not that she felt an obligation to act on his opinionated opinion.

How far had Tina sent Peter? Even if it was half-way to the Wisconsin border, she'd better work fast.

She interrupted a leggy but vacuous woman who was either discussing pool or talking dirty—her metaphors were confusing, but probably not to Tom.

"Tom, can I talk to you for a minute?"

The empty-faced woman gave her a look that suggested another use for a pool cue.

"Sure. Excuse me, uh—Candy," he said.

"Mandy," she said, already casting her eyes around the room for a new prospect.

"You're looking good," he said to Julie.

She was wearing the red dress, but it wasn't the confidence builder it had been at the wedding.

"Can we talk alone?"

"It'll be tricky. Let's see if anyone's in the bedroom."

When she hesitated, he added, "The last I saw it, the bed had about six feet of coats piled on it."

"I wasn't even thinking of that," she lied, wishing she could concentrate on something besides the way his body was a perfect fit with hers.

"What's up?" he asked when they were inside the room and Tom closed the door behind them.

"I just wanted to thank you for all your help."

"No need. I'm not at all sure I've been helpful."

He looked as uncomfortable as she felt.

"I hope you've enjoyed the tickets."

"Saw some great games."

"If you don't mind, I'd like to ask your advice one more time."

He was wearing a white chambray shirt with sleeves rolled to his elbows and the top snaps open to reveal a sexy V and a thatch of silky brown hair. His jeans hugged his thighs and didn't do much to turn off her overly active imagination. He was the only man she knew who was X-rated in ordinary clothes.

"If I mind, will you not ask?" he challenged.

"No, not if that's your attitude." She tried to get around him to the door, but he was making it difficult. In fact, he made everything difficult, and she'd started to lose her nerve even before he showed reluctance.

"Ask." He caught her elbows and held her close enough to smell his aftershave but too far away to feel the heat of his body against hers.

"Peter asked me to go to Las Vegas for a weekend. What should I do?"

He released her arms and held his own stiffly at his sides. For a moment she thought he wasn't going to answer.

"Do whatever you want to."

"I'm not sure," she confessed, needing more from him. "Isn't there some 'rule' governing this sort of thing?"

"Sorry, I'm fresh out of rules."

"Fine."

She thanked him through clenched teeth, knowing

she was defeated but still unwilling to lie down and play dead.

Neither of them moved, but he refused to meet her eyes.

"Well, thanks for nothing," she said after an awkward silence.

She didn't intend to be sarcastic. She didn't plan what happened next, but even when he scowled, his lips were full and sensual, the same ones that haunted her restless sleep. She stood on tiptoes, aiming for the little crease at the corner of his mouth but missing. Their lips connected full-on, and she kissed him as hard as she could, closing her eyes and feeling shock waves like nothing she'd ever experienced.

Then she skirted around him and found the doorknob.

"I think you should go to Vegas," he said in a tight, hard voice, making no move to stop her from leaving.

There was no other way to get through to him. She didn't know what else to say to the man who'd stiffly rejected her final offering.

She rushed from the bedroom and nearly ran into her date, back from his ice mission and looking for her.

"Peter, I've made up my mind," she said, ignoring the pain flooding through her. "I'd love to go to Las Vegas with you. Is next weekend good?"

To hell with Tom Brunswick! She was tired of his rules. From now on, she was going to make up her own.

Peter looked happy; his lips were moving, but the pain thundering through her drowned out his words.

She let him put his arm around her shoulders, forgetting how heavy it had seemed earlier.

She'd sealed her fate. Against her better judgment, she glanced over her shoulder. Tom was right behind her. He'd heard her agree to go to Vegas. The look he gave her could wilt flowers and send dogs whimpering away. She stumbled under the impact of her pain, but Peter held her tight, beginning one of his long and only occasionally witty stories.

Tom squeezed past them. She didn't see him again that evening, but he was never once out of her thoughts.

11

Julie dragged herself into her apartment late Sunday evening, wondering why she'd let Karen talk her into a consolation weekend in Wisconsin. Milwaukee in March was no substitute for sunny Vegas, especially not when it rained, sleeted or snowed most of the time. They'd gone to the art museum, seen a movie, and played a hundred games of Scrabble with Karen's aunt between heavy, home-cooked meals. The hardest part had been pretending to be cheerful.

She'd packed for Vegas early in the week, but she couldn't make herself go. Maybe she was crazy to ruin a budding friendship with a perfectly nice man, especially because of a bad boy like Tom. He had a commitment phobia bigger than the Sears Tower, and she'd finally accepted that they had no future together. Unfortunately her heart was all tangled up in her feelings for him, and it wasn't fair to encourage Peter when there was no chance she'd ever love him. He was a decent guy who didn't deserve to suffer. Only a bad girl would accept a weekend trip with no intention of getting serious, and for better or worse, she'd never be one.

Peter took it better than she'd expected. Maybe he was grateful she'd dumped him before they put an engagement announcement in the paper. He didn't have to count her as the fifth ex-fiancée.

It was possible she'd meet another nice guy down the road, but she had to recover from Tom first. She wasn't up to the emotional dishonesty of dating one man while she longed to be with another. She might meet someone nice when she got Tom out of her system, but right now it felt as if that would take forever. She could imagine herself, white-haired and elderly, finally ready for another romance but limited by the selection in the retirement home.

Her coat was in the closet and her shoes off before she noticed the blinking light on her answering machine. The indicator showed four messages. She was tempted to pull the plug and go to bed without hearing them, but there was always the off chance something had happened to her parents. She reluctantly pushed the play button.

''Julie, if you're there, pick up the phone.''

Tom. She'd know his voice anywhere. Why was he calling? She was supposed to be in Vegas with Peter. Anyway, they had absolutely nothing to say to each other.

''Julie, where the heck are you? This is Tom. It's about five o'clock.''

The next two messages were more of the same. He sounded agitated, anxious and angry. She couldn't imagine why he'd called once, let alone four times.

She dialed him at home, but got his machine. She didn't leave a message. What could she possibly say?

And what could he possibly want?

Monday morning she was putting an oversize purple bow on a funeral arrangement when Tom came through the door of the shop like a storm trooper, bomber jacket open over a black turtleneck, bearing down on her before she could recover from the shock of seeing him.

"Where have you been all weekend?"

"Where have I been?" She was too dumbfounded by the question to answer. Why did he care?

"We have to talk," he said loudly enough to bring her boss out from the back room.

"Is there a problem?" the older woman asked.

"No problem," Julie quickly assured her, "but if you don't mind, I'll take my lunch break now."

"I would if I were you," her boss said knowingly, apparently not immune to bad-boy tactics even though she had three grandchildren.

Julie had the crazy idea Tom would throw her over his shoulder and carry her out if she didn't hurry. She grabbed her coat and purse with him on her heels as though she might try to duck out the back way. He literally dragged her out of the shop, his arm around her shoulders so she practically had to run to keep up.

"Why are you doing this?" she sputtered, more flabbergasted than angry at his high-handed abduction.

He opened the door of his van, illegally parked right in front of the door.

"Get in—please."

"Where are we going? What is this all about?"

"You're the one who has a lot of explaining to do."

"About what?" She was practically wailing, torn between getting mad and lapsing into hysterical giggles. "Tom, answer me!"

He didn't drive far, and he didn't say much. He stopped at a small strip mall with trendy clothing shops, a Chinese restaurant and a jewelry shop. He parked in the row closest to the jewelry shop.

"I'm not getting out of this van until you tell me what's going on," she said.

"Sure you are." He smiled for the first time, a wicked grin that made her feel hot needles in her nether regions.

"No, I mean it!"

He threw open the door on the passenger side, reached across her lap to release the seat belt and picked her up—literally—sliding one arm under her legs and the other behind her.

"Put me down!" Talk about feeling like the village idiot! She wrapped her arms around his neck, not at all sure he wouldn't drop her.

"Promise to come along quietly?"

For some reason she couldn't fathom, he seemed to be enjoying himself immensely.

She shook her head and he put her down, then he took her hand and pulled her into the jewelry store.

"We'd like to look at engagement rings," he told the clerk, totally astonishing Julie. "That tray looks pretty good," he said, pointing through the glass case.

He sat on one of the velvet-upholstered stools provided for customers and hugged her against him.

"Pick one out—unless I'm too late," he said matter-of-factly. "The one you like best. I don't care what it costs."

He lifted her left hand and examined her naked ring finger, seemingly satisfied.

"What on earth are you doing?" Her heart was racing; she was breathless with excitement. This couldn't be happening! She'd overslept, and this was a wild fantasy existing only in her dreams.

"I'm proposing. What does it look like? That one's nice." He pointed at a huge solitaire, more diamond than she could imagine wearing.

"We haven't even had a real first date yet!"

The bald, middle-aged clerk stopped taking out trays, looking as confused as she felt.

"We can skip the preliminaries. We'll play by my rules now," Tom said.

"What rules? You don't want to get married!"

"Are you sure?"

The look he gave her could melt butter. It only lasted an instant, but it showed her a whole different side of him—goofy, love-struck, and impetuous.

"Slow down a minute. Please! Let me catch up." She was as confused as she was happy.

He glanced at the jeweler, apparently deciding to ignore him for the moment, and stood, taking both her hands in his.

"I flew to Las Vegas this weekend to persuade you not to marry Peter. I checked every hotel on the strip and nearly freaked when I couldn't find you. Don't tell me you didn't get my messages!"

"Yes, four of them. You thought I was going to marry Peter?"

"Well, Tina said she heard…why go to Vegas if you weren't planning a quickie wedding in one of those cheesy chapels? Yeah—I checked those out, too."

"You big dope!" she said affectionately. "Peter won the trip for being top salesperson. He was going to get a separate room for me, but I didn't go. Did you really fly to Vegas to stop me?"

He looked ready to eat her for breakfast.

"What did you say?" His eyes were burning holes in her.

"Peter won the trip—"

"No, fast forward to the part about not going."

"I didn't go."

"You didn't go?"

"No."

He calmed down from a mini-tornado to a sheepish boy caught with his hand in the cookie jar. She didn't know which she loved most.

"Why do a crazy thing like that—going after me?" she asked.

The clerk replaced the ring trays and retired to the far end of the store, at least pretending not to be eavesdropping.

"Why, Tom?" She had to know. Her whole future depended on him fessing up. Maybe she wouldn't have to wait for a nice octogenarian in the distant future, after all.

He was tongue-tied. She wouldn't have believed it if she hadn't seen it.

"We don't have to talk here," she said softly, this time leading him out of the store.

"Back here," he said hoarsely, sliding open the middle door of his van and giving her his hand as she stepped up to the seat.

He got in beside her and slammed the door shut.

"When I thought you were eloping with Peter," he said hesitantly, taking both her hands in his, "I realized...I was afraid...I thought I might lose you forever."

"I'm never going to marry Peter. I don't love him.

But you never wanted to be tied down to one woman.''

"Not any woman I knew before I met you.''

He leaned toward her and finally did what he should have done eons ago. He kissed her with all the love in his heart.

His lips brushed gently against hers, teasing them apart until an emotional dam broke and their mouths came together without restraint.

"I love you,'' he said, the words coming from deep in his throat.

She'd never heard anything so beautiful.

"I want you.'' His hand was on her leg, between her legs, his mouth hot on her throat, his breath warm and tickling.

"But I don't want to spend our honeymoon in jail,'' he said, taking a deep shuddering breath and moving away. "There's only so much we can do in a parking lot.''

"Tom…''

"I can't live without you, Julie.''

"You don't have to.''

"I'll do anything to be with you. I've tortured myself long enough, pretending I'm worth anything without you. I'm ready to pick out china patterns, rent a tux, do the bit with rice.…''

"Tom, please don't—''

"Don't tell you I love you?''

"No—yes. I mean, do tell me, do love me!'' She brought his hand to her lips and kissed his fingers, wanting to hold on to some part of him to assure herself this was really happening. "But I don't want you to marry me.''

"I want to—''

"No! It's too quick—you don't have to! Don't rush into something you'll regret, something you don't really want, just because…''

"Because I'm crazy about you, and I'm going to die if I don't make love to you almost immediately?''

"I'll take a long lunch hour.''

"Take the rest of the day off.''

She smiled, feeling as though she was about to be transformed into a better, finer person.

Three days later she still felt as though she were riding a carousel that never stopped. She was giddy with happiness and so crazy in love she didn't think a lifetime would be long enough to get used to being with Tom.

"What do you think of it?'' He carried her through the doorway of their Las Vegas room and across to the quilted satin surface of the king-size bed.

"It's wonderful!'' She wasn't talking about the room with its brocade drapes and white French Provincial furniture.

"Now, Mrs. Brunswick,'' he said, quickly closing the door, "what would you like to do first?''

"Um—play roulette. Definitely play roulette.''

"Roulette.'' He made the word sound erotic. "First a proper wedding kiss.''

"Another one of your rules?'' She stood and leaned against him, still amazed at how wonderful he looked in a charcoal suit and a red paisley tie.

"No more rules.''

He kissed her deeply, seriously, his fingers busy with the buttons on her white linen suit jacket. Under it she was wearing only a lacy bra, and he plucked at one cup until his fingers embraced the naked swell of her breast.

"You don't mind tying the knot in a marriage mill, do you?" he asked.

"It wasn't so bad. At least the flowers were silk, not plastic."

He discarded her bra as quickly as he had her jacket, then slid her short skirt and panty hose down her legs. It was incredibly arousing to stand naked in the arms of a man in a suit, especially when that man was Tom.

"Do you think our families will ever forgive us for eloping?" she asked, weak with the need to surrender herself totally to sensation as his hands caressed her shoulders and back.

"Had to elope…no time to find a dress."

He started doing something wonderful with his tongue, at the same time dropping his hands lower, fondling her bottom until she almost danced with eagerness.

"It's possible to find one on short notice. You proved that." But it wasn't possible to think with his tongue teasing her nipple and his hand sliding between her legs, parting them….

"They'll get even," he promised. "They'll party us until we beg for mercy."

"It'll be fun."

But nothing would ever be as much fun as making love with Tom. She didn't need experience to know he was wonderful—gentle the first time when she needed him to be, playful when she was tense, eager when she was ready. Their first time together in her apartment, he'd been humble with gratitude, stunned that he was her first—and he vowed her last—lover.

"Mrs. Brunswick." He said it with awe, like a mystical incantation. "My wife, my love."

"Haven't you forgotten something?" She reached out and parted his shirt, opening buttons with fingers made deft by desire.

He undressed quickly, his body still a wonder to her—firm, and strong with beguiling soft spots and places she could touch to reduce him to frantic eagerness. She'd lost track of how many times he'd melded his body with hers, each time deepening her pleasure and stoking fires she never expected to be extinguished.

Every time with Julie was like his first time, only infinitely more satisfying. He wanted her now even more than he had after they left the jewelry shop—was it really only three days ago? Time seemed to stand still for them, one continual festival of longing and loving.

He pulled her onto the bed and kissed her until her lips were ringed with the pinkness of passion and her wonderful pinkish-brown nipples were hard. He never knew what to expect; one minute she had to be coaxed, pulling a sheet to her chin and making a game of his urgency; the next she reached out to him, more exciting and erotic than he'd ever dreamed possible. He regretted every single night of his life not spent making love to her.

He was totally sure he'd done the right thing in marrying her so quickly. He couldn't imagine life without her. She was gorgeous, sexy, alluring—and the nicest woman he'd ever met. He still got cold sweats when he realized how close he'd come to losing her. Knowing she was really his was like looking at the world with new eyes. Maybe his euphoria wouldn't last, but his love would. There was nothing he wanted more than to make her happy.

He rose over her, satisfied for the moment to admire her exquisite beauty—the smoothness of her skin, the lushness of her breasts, her graceful limbs and sleek little belly. When he parted her legs, he wanted to howl with happiness at her response. How could he possibly have known her more than a day without doing everything in his power to make her his?

Being inside her was like nothing he'd ever experienced. One moment she seemed lost in sensations; the next she caressed his manhood or ran her nails lightly over his buttocks. With any other woman, these were only erotic tricks, but there was so much love in Julie's touch that he was humbled, grateful and aroused more deeply than he'd ever dreamed possible.

"I love you." He couldn't say it enough, but when, sooner than he'd expected, her stunning climax triggered his own, he couldn't stop saying it.

"I love you. I love you. I love you."

He cradled her against his chest, drowsy but not wanting to sleep, knowing how little rest he needed to be ready to make love to her again.

The wonder of it was, what happened between them wasn't just sex or any of the other terms he'd been using most of his life. He could only call it making love because that was what it was.

Later, much later, they lay, legs entwined, her hair dark and glossy on his chest and her hand resting lightly on his shoulder.

He lifted her hand and looked at the sparkling solitaire—one diamond to represent one lifelong marriage, she called it—and the simple gold band she'd chosen, both more modest than he'd been willing to give her but more beautiful on her small hand than he could have imagined.

"Do you like your ring?" he asked, nuzzling her knuckles.

She admired it for a moment, then raised her head and smiled at him with heartwarming joy on her face.

"I love it, but I love you much more. You didn't have to marry me, you know."

"I've probably made a terrible mistake," he teased.

"I'm serious, Tom. I'd stay with you forever without any ties. I'd sleep with you—"

"You already did. I didn't marry you to get into your panties."

"Stop that!" She playfully slapped his hand when he tried to distract her, and sat up, leaning over him until her hair tickled his nose.

"I'd be happy just dating you," she said earnestly. "You didn't have to rush into marriage. I don't want you to be sorry—ever."

"We had to get married. It's in the rule book."

"What rule book?" She tweaked his nose but made up for it with a kiss that sent flaming arrows shooting downward.

"The one I plan to write. *How to Meet and Marry Ms. Right,*" he said, pulling her closer. "I had to marry you."

"Because I compromised your honor?"

Spoken like a true bad-girl bride.

"Because I love you too much to let you get snapped up by some geek like what's-his-name."

"I can't believe it. You're jealous!"

"Not anymore."

He rolled over on top of her, wondering if maybe once more—no, definitely once more.

"I love you." They said it simultaneously.

"Married only a few hours, and already we're thinking alike," she said, doing a little wiggle that drove him nuts.

"Roulette now?" he teased.

"We're the only people here who will go home richer without ever playing."

*   *   *   *   *

HER PASSION FOR DR JONES by Lilian Darcy
Southshore - No.1 of 4

Dr Harry Jones is sure it's a mistake having Rebecca Irwin work in the practice. Despite the raging attraction between her and Harry, Rebecca fought her corner!

BACHELOR CURE by Marion Lennox
Bachelor Doctors

Dr Tessa Westcott burst into Mike Llewellyn's life like a red-headed whirlwind. She said exactly what she thought, and turned his ordered world upside down. It couldn't last. But Mike had to admit, she lightened his life.

HOLDING THE BABY by Laura MacDonald

Lewis's sister was abroad and he was left holding the baby—literally! He *badly* needed help with the three children and asked Jo Henry to be nanny. In a family situation, Jo and Lewis became *vividly* aware of each other...

SEVENTH DAUGHTER by Gill Sanderson

Specialist registrar Dr James Owen was everything Dr Delyth Price ever wanted in a man. But Delyth had a gift not everyone understood. James seemed prepared to listen, if not to believe. Then she discovered his lighthearted side, and fell even deeper into love...

Spoil yourself next month
with these four novels from

TEMPTATION

MACKENZIE'S WOMAN by JoAnn Ross

Bachelor Auction

Kate Campbell had to persuade Alec Mackenzie to take part in a
charity bachelor auction. This rugged adventurer would have
women bidding millions for an hour of his time. Trouble was,
Alec wasn't really a bachelor. Though nobody knew it—he was
married to Kate!

A PRIVATE EYEFUL by Ruth Jean Dale

Hero for Hire

Nick Charles was a bodyguard on a vital assignment. But no one
had yet told him exactly what that assignment was! So he was
hanging around a luxury resort, waiting… Then along came
luscious Cory Leblanc and Nick just knew she was a prime
candidate—for *something*…

PRIVATE LESSONS by Julie Elizabeth Leto

Blaze

'Harley' turned up on Grant Riordan's doorstep and sent his
libido skyrocketing. Hired as the 'entertainment' for a bachelor
party, she was dressed like an exotic dancer but had the eyes of
an innocent. Unfortunately, after a little accident, she didn't
have a clue who she was…

SEDUCING SYDNEY by Kathy Marks

Plain-Jane Sydney Stone was feeling seriously out of place in a
glamorous Las Vegas hotel, when she received a mysterious
note arranging a date—for that night! She was sure the message
must have been delivered to the wrong woman. But maybe
she'd just go and find out…

Our hottest
TEMPTATION
authors bring you...

Blaze

**Three sizzling love stories available in
one volume in September 1999.**

Midnight Heat
JoAnn Ross

A Lark in the Dark
Heather MacAllister

Night Fire
Elda Minger

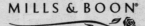

FREE!

4 Books
and a surprise gift!

We would like to take this opportunity to thank you for reading this Mills & Boon® book by offering you the chance to take FOUR more specially selected titles from the Presents...™ series absolutely FREE! We're also making this offer to introduce you to the benefits of the Reader Service™—

★ FREE home delivery
★ FREE gifts and competitions
★ FREE monthly Newsletter
★ Books available before they're in the shops
★ Exclusive Reader Service discounts

Accepting these FREE books and gift places you under no obligation to buy; you may cancel at any time, even after receiving your free shipment. Simply complete your details below and return the entire page to the address below. **You don't even need a stamp!**

YES! Please send me 4 free Presents...™ books and a surprise gift. I understand that unless you hear from me, I will receive 6 superb new titles every month for just £2.40 each, postage and packing free. I am under no obligation to purchase any books and may cancel my subscription at any time. The free books and gift will be mine to keep in any case.

P9EB

Ms/Mrs/Miss/Mr ....Initials..............................

BLOCK CAPITALS PLEASE

Surname..

Address...

....

....Postcode ....

Send this whole page to:
THE READER SERVICE, FREEPOST CN81, CROYDON, CR9 3WZ
(Eire readers please send coupon to: P.O. BOX 4546, KILCOCK, COUNTY KILDARE)

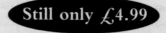